They had company.

A.J. wondered if Gabrielle had any idea just how much trouble she was in. He immersed himself in the underbrush, like a sniper taking cover. A.J. pulled the foliage in around him and sat stone still. His tension didn't ease until the group that had been following Gabrielle had taken the bait and followed the wrong trail. He was thankful for his training, that he could keep her safe.

When enough time had passed, he surfaced from his hiding place and headed after his target. Reaching Gabrielle was critical now.

A single second could mean the difference between life and death. For her and the children...

DEBRA WEBB

RAW TALENT

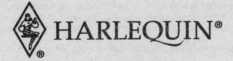

HARLEQUIN®

TORONTO • NEW YORK • LONDON
AMSTERDAM • PARIS • SYDNEY • HAMBURG
STOCKHOLM • ATHENS • TOKYO • MILAN • MADRID
PRAGUE • WARSAW • BUDAPEST • AUCKLAND

Life sometimes throws us painful curves. We can learn from them and move on with our lives or we can allow the past to jeopardize our future. This book is dedicated to a man who has overcome the obstacles life has tossed in his way. He has risen above numerous adversities and remained ever hopeful. To my baby brother, John Brashier, with all my love, this one is for you.

ISBN 0-373-22916-X

RAW TALENT

Copyright © 2006 by Debra Webb

www.eHarlequin.com

Printed in U.S.A.

ABOUT THE AUTHOR

Debra Webb was born in Scottsboro, Alabama, to parents who taught her that anything is possible if you want it badly enough. She began writing at age nine. Eventually she met and married the man of her dreams, and tried some other occupations, including selling vacuum cleaners, working in a factory, a day-care center, a hospital and a department store. When her husband joined the military, they moved to Berlin, Germany, and Debra became a secretary in the commanding general's office. By 1985 they were back in the States, and finally moved to Tennessee, to a small town where everyone knows everyone else. With the support of her husband and two beautiful daughters, Debra took up writing again, looking to mystery and movies for inspiration. In 1998, her dream of writing for Harlequin came true. You can write to Debra with your comments at P.O. Box 64, Huntland, Tennessee 37345 or visit her Web site at http://www.debrawebb.com to find out exciting news about her next book.

Books by Debra Webb

HARLEQUIN INTRIGUE

583—SAFE BY HIS SIDE*
597—THE BODYGUARD'S BABY*
610—PROTECTIVE CUSTODY*
634—SPECIAL ASSIGNMENT: BABY
646—SOLITARY SOLDIER*
659—PERSONAL PROTECTOR*
671—PHYSICAL EVIDENCE*
683—CONTRACT BRIDE*
693—UNDERCOVER WIFE**
697—HER HIDDEN TRUTH**
701—GUARDIAN OF THE NIGHT**
718—HER SECRET ALIBI*
732—KEEPING BABY SAFE*
747—CRIES IN THE NIGHT*
768—AGENT COWBOY*

801—SITUATION: OUT OF CONTROL†
807—FULL EXPOSURE†
837—JOHN DOE ON HER DOORSTEP††
843—EXECUTIVE BODYGUARD††
849—MAN OF HER DREAMS††
864—URBAN SENSATION
891—PERSON OF INTEREST
909—INVESTIGATING 101‡
915—RAW TALENT‡

*Colby Agency
**The Specialists
†Colby Agency: Internal Affairs
††The Enforcers
‡Colby Agency: New Recruits

CAST OF CHARACTERS

Gabrielle Jordan—She is one of the Colby Agency's new recruits, but she isn't who she says she is. She has one goal: revenge.

A. J. Braddock—He is one of the Colby Agency's newest and hottest investigators. He is an expert tracker. If anyone can find Gabrielle before she completes her mission, he can.

Trevor Sloan—Sloan has been to hell and back more than once. He will not allow anyone to threaten his family under any circumstances.

Pablo Vencino—Sloan's most trusted employee.

Valerie Vencino—Pablo's niece, who learns the hard way that love is blind.

Manuel Estes—Valerie's untrustworthy boyfriend who will do anything for money.

Detective Hernando Cervantes—He knows there is more to this case than a mere kidnapping.

Chico Vega—An old contact of Sloan's who can provide anyone with anything most anywhere.

George Fuentes—A man who likes his business and doesn't intend to let anyone get in his way.

Chapter One

Florescitaf, Mexico

The cantina looked exactly like the sort of dump Gabrielle Jordan had expected. Based on what she'd read and heard about Sloan, he would fit in at Los Laureles just fine. Her jaw clenched automatically at the very thought of the man who had killed her father. A man who cared for little but himself. She didn't have to go inside the place he'd once frequented to know the clientele would be every bit as sleazy as the rundown building looked.

An alley sliced between the cantina and an open air meat market next door. The alley as well as the market appeared deserted and about as welcoming as the rest of this side of town. But that was okay. She wasn't here to make friends or to even tour the sights and sounds of a part of Mexico sheltered from the passage of time.

She was here to settle a score.

She'd traveled all this way to do one thing and one thing only: to watch a man die a slow, painful death.

No matter if she died in the process. No matter how much pain she had to endure to make it happen. She wasn't leaving until one of them was dead, him or her.

The odor of stale cigarette smoke, alcohol and plain old male sweat met her at the entrance to the cantina. Ancient overhead fans that had long ago seen better days stirred the thick air.

She moved fully into the cantina, feeling the suspicious stares cast her way like razors sliding over her skin. Tables were scattered around the room. Only a few were occupied, but that handful looked meaner than junkyard dogs. The dubious glares quickly evolved into lustful leers that made her shudder inwardly with revulsion. But she wasn't afraid. Not for a second. If any of these scumbags thought for a second that their ogling would scare her off, they had another thought coming.

Nothing scared Gabrielle. Nothing at all. A girl didn't spend eighteen months in a Texas prison without getting tough. Not to mention she'd existed her entire adult life for this destiny. No one would get in her way.

Ignoring the audience of onlookers, Gabrielle strode up to the bar and propped against its worn smooth top. "You speak English?" she asked of the man drying glasses behind the bar. He was sixty if he was a day.

"*Sí*. What is your pleasure, *señorita?*"

The dingy apron scarcely reached around his considerable girth. His thick dark hair gleamed with the slightest peppering of gray. The wide mustache made her think of old Western movies and the *commancheros* depicted through clichés exactly like this guy.

"Tequila."

"*Sí.*"

He set a tumbler on the bar then filled it without once taking his scrutinizing gaze off her.

Like the others scattered around the room, the bartender would be not only suspicious, but also curious as to her business in town. Tourists were easy to spot. Those watching her had probably figured out by now that she was not a tourist. No mere tourist would stumble into a place like this without running like hell to get right back out the swinging door.

"You come for *Cinco de Mayo?*" The bartender set the bottle of tequila aside and studied her even more closely as he waited for her response.

Gabrielle downed the shot, relishing the hot burn as it slithered like a wildfire down her throat. "No." She didn't see the point in lying. She wasn't here for any sort of festival. She was here for Sloan. "I'm looking for someone."

The old man reached for another freshly washed glass and slowly turned it in his hands, wiping away the moisture from its recent rinsing.

Gabrielle tapped her glass to prompt the pouring of

another shot. "His name is Sloan. Trevor Sloan. Have you heard of him?"

The bartender tensed noticeably as the tequila splashed into the glass. He shook his head. "I do not know of this man."

She knew he lied. She'd asked around and though only one person had admitted to recognizing the name Sloan, the woman had told Gabrielle to ask at this cantina.

Gabrielle cradled the glass for a moment before indulging her thirst. When it came to good tequila, one shot was never enough. "That's not the way I heard it." She stared directly into the man's eyes, let him see her unyielding determination. "I understand you know him quite well."

He slung the drying cloth over his shoulder, shelved the clean glass behind him, before leaning across the bar toward her. "What is your business with Mr. Sloan?" he inquired quietly, as if it was not safe to speak of the subject in public. The suspicion in his eyes had evolved into something along the lines of anger.

Gabrielle wasn't intimidated. She inclined her head and met that lethal glare head-on. "It's personal."

His gaze narrowed. "Personal can be dangerous, *señorita*."

She smiled; the reflection captured in the mirror behind the bar wasn't pleasant, she noted in her peripheral vision. Good. She wanted him to know she didn't like his games. "You'll either tell me where I can find him, or you won't. But don't waste my time, *señor*." She said the last with a warning tone of her own.

Sloan had obviously made himself a few friends in town. Or, maybe, they were all afraid of him. She didn't really care which it was, she simply wanted an answer to her question.

How the hell did she find him if she couldn't get anyone to talk?

The file she'd taken from the Colby Agency hadn't given his specific address, just the general vicinity. She'd spent twenty-four hours checking out the surrounding area with no luck at all. Flat-out asking about his whereabouts carried a significant risk, but she was tired of wasting her time. She needed a location. Now. Today. No more playing hide-and-seek. Not to mention someone at the Colby Agency would likely warn Sloan the moment her breach was discovered. Time was not on her side.

The bartender turned his back on her and went about the business of checking his stock of liquors.

Gabrielle swore under her breath. Another dead end. There had to be someone around here willing to give her a location.

"What do I owe you?" No point hanging around in this seedy joint and killing more time. He'd made his decision and she wasn't going to change his mind.

The bartender shifted slightly, just far enough to make eye contact with her. "You owe me *nothing*."

Nothing? What was the deal with this guy? She reached into the pocket of her jeans and dragged out an adequate number of pesos. Whatever this guy's problem, she wasn't about to leave owing him a damned thing. She slapped the money on the bar. "That should do it."

He glanced at the payment then at her. "Your money is no good here, *señorita*."

Now she was plain old ticked off. "Why the hell not?"

He faced her squarely, braced his hands on the counter and looked deeply into her eyes, his intent unreadable. "I do not accept payment from the dead."

Never one to squander her hard-earned cash, Gabrielle snatched up the money and walked out. She didn't spare a glance for any of the scumbags staring after her. To hell with all of them. She wasn't beaten yet.

All she had to do was to stick with it. In her experience, patience and persistence paid off. She would find Sloan. Maybe not today. But soon.

And then she would kill him.

Just like she'd dreamed of for three long years.

Some girls fantasized about their first date or their first kiss, maybe the first prom. Not Gabrielle. Ever since she'd been old enough to understand what betrayal and murder really meant, she'd dreamed of finding her father's killer and having her revenge.

She'd survived a childhood in pure hell, with a drunken mother who had given her just one thing: the understanding of why her life had stunk from the moment she'd been born.

Gabrielle's father had been a special investigator for the State Department. He'd traveled extensively, hadn't even been there when his only daughter was born. His work had turned particularly ugly, forcing him to, in effect, abandon his only child, to protect her. But he'd called, her mother had insisted, once in a great while when it was safe. If he'd ever sent money, Gabrielle's mother had blown it on booze.

And then, just before Gabrielle's eighteenth birthday, the calls had stopped, according to her mother. It wasn't until she'd graduated high school a few months later and was poised to enter college on an academic scholarship that Gabrielle had learned the truth of what happened. An old enemy had murdered her father. The State Department had disowned him. The newspapers had called him an assassin, a cold-blooded killer. Gabrielle hadn't needed her mother's pathetic ramblings to know what that meant. She remembered watching a television interview once about a man who had given his all to his country and then been abandoned to cover their involvement in certain activities. Her father had deserved better. So had she.

Her mother had fallen even more deeply into her depressive state and then promptly proceeded to drink herself to death, literally. Gabrielle had buried her the day before she'd been supposed to head for college.

She'd realized something painful as shovel full after shovel full of dirt had been tossed atop her mother's cheap coffin. She was alone. Completely alone. That was when the need for vengeance had begun to eat at her like a rapidly spreading disease.

She'd gone off to college as planned, but sticking to that hard-earned and long-awaited agenda for her future had fallen by the wayside as she'd formed a new goal. Obsessed about it really.

Find her father's killer and make him pay.

Her new goal hadn't actually formulated so clearly or easily…at least not at first. She'd tried to put the past behind her. She'd truly attempted to focus on her studies but luck had, apparently, been against her all along. She hadn't made encouraging friends. The only acceptance she had found was with those who'd grown up much as she had, with absent or pathetic excuses for parents and a lack of funds. Maybe that was the reason her bitterness had taken such deep roots. Her mother's words had haunted her and her new friends' cynicism had nurtured her growing hatred for the raw deal life had dealt her.

Thus her new determination had been born. Make the man responsible for her final kick in the teeth pay.

As far as Gabrielle was concerned, the man, Sloan, was responsible not only for her father's death, but for her mother's, as well. Not that her mother had ever been much of a parent, but she'd been all Gabrielle had in the world. Sloan had taken that away from her.

Gabrielle doubted she would survive the coming face-off to get on with her life, but maybe that was her true destiny. This business would have been finished two years ago if she hadn't been framed by a so-called friend. She'd spent eighteen months doing time for someone else's stupidity. She'd tried to fight it at first, but with no money and her only legal counsel having been assigned by the court, she'd pretty much been screwed from the outset. So, she'd sucked it up and done the time. Used it as a learning experience, a chance to hone her focus. If she could survive prison, she could do this. *No problema.*

All she had to do was find the bastard known as Sloan.

Someone around here would slip up and give her the information she needed. She wouldn't give up until she had the information she needed.

Both her mother and her father had allowed life to get in the way of a decent relationship with their daughter. Their combined shortfalls had forged a strength in her that was relentless. One she hadn't recognized herself until a few months ago. She would not allow anything to get in her way. She wanted to do something right just once. And this would be it.

Sloan was dead already.

He just didn't know it yet.

Chapter Two

A.J. Braddock had worked at the Colby Agency a short time, but during that brief stint he had learned many things. For one, Victoria Colby-Camp never misread a client. She hired only the very best in the business of private investigations and her ability to make things happen was uncanny.

But in the past twenty-four hours everything had changed.

Gabrielle Jordan, aka Gabrielle Hanson, had fooled everyone, including the invincible Victoria.

The twenty-two-year-old woman had hired on as a new recruit, had performed exceedingly well during her short training, and then promptly disappeared, with a sensitive Colby Agency file in tow.

Whatever the young lady's story, she was in serious trouble. Not with the authorities, A.J. considered, but with Victoria. No one double-crossed the head of the Colby Agency and got off scot-free. No. Victoria would make this right if it was the last thing she did. That was the other thing about his boss that A.J. admired so, she was fiercely determined.

An emergency meeting of the staff had been held a few hours ago and A.J. had been appointed the task of tracking down Gabrielle Jordan and bringing her back to face Victoria.

Several others, Simon Ruhl and Ian Michaels included, had wanted the assignment but, using her usual astute judgment, Victoria had recognized the need for total objectivity.

The way A.J. understood the situation, most everyone at the Colby Agency knew Trevor Sloan, or at least had been living with tales of his legendary story for years. To that end, all concerned felt extremely loyal to the man and would do whatever necessary to see that he suffered no additional drama in his life.

Trevor Sloan had lost one family, had almost given up on life in general, when a woman and her son resurrected him. Sloan had not only found love again, but he had also discovered that the son he'd thought long dead was, in fact, alive and well. Victoria would allow nothing to interfere with Sloan's newfound happiness.

However, in typical fashion, the boss also understood that Gabrielle Jordan had a story of her own. Once she broke her cover, it didn't take the agency long to get the story on her. The young woman deserved the opportunity to know the full truth and to resume her life without the bitter, ugly baggage of the past.

In A.J.'s opinion, Gabrielle Jordan needed a wake-up call—Marine style. But first and foremost, he had to find her and stop her emotionally charged plunge into self-destruction.

Trevor Sloan was no one to mess with. He'd been to hell and back a couple of times and he likely had no desire to return. He wouldn't let anyone threaten his new family or his hard-earned happiness.

A.J. felt confident he could handle the situation. He'd worked closely with the new recruits Victoria had hired last month. Todd Thompson had proven his worth on the job. His ambitiousness had, at times, been tedious, but he'd come through in the end. Victoria had chosen well.

Gabrielle had actually been the one A.J. had assumed would stand out from the small herd of new recruits. She'd proven resourceful, dedicated and anxious to make her place here at the Colby Agency.

If he was entirely honest with himself, he'd admit that she had earned more than his professional respect. He'd been attracted to her from day one. How could he not be? Gabrielle had a fire in her that burned with such heat he couldn't help being drawn to her. She wanted to learn, wanted to be the best. He'd admired those qualities.

Her beauty hadn't helped the situation. Ignoring how gorgeous she was would have been completely outside the realm of reason. Long black hair, gray eyes that reminded him of glittering silver in the sunlight.

Not once had he allowed their time together to move beyond the bounds of a working relationship. He knew better. The military had long ago drilled that rule into his head. Fraternization was against the rules.

He'd figured he would get past the little infatuation. Hell, he hadn't been involved with anyone in too long to talk about. He should have seen this one coming, but he hadn't. Now, here he was, charged with the duty of going after her and bringing her back.

He could do it. And maybe it was better this way. Those weaker emotions, the ones he attempted to keep in check, likely needed this lesson in futility. He had to remember where he stood in the grand scheme of things. He could not permit close personal relationships. It wasn't as if he didn't understand the situation.

All he had to do was to remember the deal—like it or not.

As the door to Victoria's office opened, A.J. stood to greet the woman herself. He booted all other lingering thoughts from his head and focused on the realities. He had a job to do. End of story.

"Good evening, A.J." She smiled. "Please, sit."

As she strode around her desk to her own chair he noted that she looked as elegant and calm as ever. One would never know that the agency was in the middle of a major crisis.

He settled back into his chair as she did into her own. "I'm ready to leave immediately. I've taken the liberty of arranging air as well as ground transportation. My flight leaves in three hours." It was the earliest flight he could get with one stop too many, but it was better than waiting until tomorrow.

"I appreciate your preparedness, A.J. But let's have Elaine cancel your arrangements for the sake of time and convenience. The agency jet will take you to a private airfield near Florescitaf where ground transportation will be waiting."

Surprised, A.J. acknowledged the change with a nod. "Outstanding. I can be ready within the hour." He wasn't going to argue with private transport. He just hadn't expected to be allowed such a privilege. His experience in the Marines was that only those who had achieved a certain level and paid their dues were permitted the most advantageous perks. He had to remember that the private sector did things a little differently. It would take some getting used to. Elaine, the agency's receptionist, would take good care of him.

Victoria passed a manila folder across her desk to him. "Your mission is fairly straightforward, as you know. Find her and bring her back. She won't like it, but if she wishes to avoid official charges, she will be cooperative."

The file contained all the pertinent information the agency had on Gabrielle, which wasn't that much, but it was enough background for A.J.'s needs. He already knew her, understood how she thought to a degree.

He closed the folder and fixed his gaze on the woman waiting for any questions. "I need to understand just how far you want me to go in order to stop Miss Jordan's plans for vengeance." In spite of his efforts, he found himself failing to breathe as he waited for her response.

Victoria held his gaze for several seconds before answering. During that time he saw a glimmer of uncertainty in her eyes. That surprised him. He'd never once known her to waiver, would have wagered against it. He couldn't tell if her hesitation was a good thing or a bad one as far as Gabrielle's fate was concerned.

"Miss Jordan is operating under many misconceptions that make her judgment unreliable. My preference would be for you to intervene and, without significant incident, bring her back here." She paused a moment, seemed to drag up her courage. "However, preventing her from reaching Sloan and his family is priority one."

Her expression turned grave as she went on. "If she reaches him, her fate is out of our hands. I would prefer that didn't happen. I've tried without success to contact Sloan or his household helper Pablo. If we're lucky, he and his family are away. But he could return any moment." Victoria pressed A.J. with a look that conveyed a great deal more than her words. "I need you to do whatever it takes, A.J. We have to stop this train crash before it happens, if at all possible."

The decision was made. He had his orders. Personal feelings had no place beyond this point.

"I understand. I won't use excessive force unless absolutely necessary, but I won't hesitate should the need arise."

Victoria nodded. "We're in agreement then."

"I'll report in as often as possible." He pushed to his feet.

"We'll keep you posted with any information we gather on this end."

A.J. nodded once before turning to the door. Every second he wasted was one that might cost Gabrielle Jordan far more than she wanted to pay. That was one way in which he could help her in all this.

"One last thing, A.J."

He hesitated at the door and faced Victoria again. "Yes?"

She stood behind her desk, that atypical uncertainty haunting her expression once more. "You're certain you feel comfortable with this?"

He wasn't entirely surprised by her question. It pained her to ask. That much was clear. Also very clear was her reasoning, elaborating was in no way necessary. "I'm one hundred percent certain, ma'am."

Drawing in a deep breath, she nodded once, banishing the uncertainty he'd seen in her expression. "Very well then. Based on your experience and your objectivity in the matter, I am of the opinion that you are the best man for the job. However, if you feel the need for backup, all it takes is one call. I'll leave that to your discretion."

"I understand."

"Of course it will be best if I can contact Sloan ahead of your arrival," she went on, apparently only then deciding to mention this part. "In the event that doesn't work out, tell him that I'm trusting him to do the right thing on this. Even pure evil can occasionally spawn something good. He'll know what I mean."

A.J. left Victoria's office with only a vague idea what her message to Sloan meant, but he felt no need to question her orders. He had learned well from his career in the military that there were times when a soldier didn't need to know every detail about a mission. He simply needed the know-how and the determination to carry out the assignment.

Knowledge was a very powerful tool, no doubt. But, at times, knowledge could be a stumbling block to achieving the greater good.

This was one of those situations.

He appreciated that Victoria practiced what she preached. She had complete faith in his ability to get the job done. To his relief, much of that faith was based on his word. He strongly believed that a man was only as good as his word. It pleased him that his new employer shared that belief.

Just another reason he couldn't allow any personal

feelings he'd foolishly allowed to develop to get in his way of doing his job. He needed his work, needed that kind of focus in his life. There wasn't room for anything else. Not anymore. He had to keep that truth in mind and stop permitting wishful thinking from overriding good sense.

A.J. considered his plan of action as he stopped by his town house for his bags and drove to the airfield where the Colby Agency jet would be waiting.

Picking up Jordan's trail wouldn't be difficult. Florescitaf was a small village and an attractive young urban woman would stand out. Since she didn't know the location of Sloan's private residence, she would have to ask questions or go on a grid search of the surrounding area. Either way would be time-consuming as well as risky as far as keeping a low profile.

Once on board the agency jet, he used his time to brush up on his Spanish. He hadn't used the language in ages, but getting his point across wouldn't be difficult. An hour later he felt confident with his spotty vocabulary so he took some time to consider his target.

Gabrielle Jordan was very young, only twenty-two. She'd spent eighteen months of that young life in prison. The first six months of that time she'd made a fuss about being innocent, including writing several appeals herself, none of which were taken seriously by her court-appointed attorney. So she'd shut up and done her time.

She'd gotten out only a few months before applying

for a job at the Colby Agency. Her ability to create a false identity was commendable if misguided. She hadn't missed a trick. Case in point, she'd fooled one of the top private investigation agencies in the country.

He had to smile. The woman had herself some real brass ones, that was for sure. He closed the door on that line of thinking. From what they'd learned in the past twenty-four hours, she was the only child of an alcoholic mother who claimed Gabriel DiCassi as the child's father. DiCassi had been Trevor Sloan's arch enemy and an international assassin. A standoff between the two men had ended in DiCassi's death.

Apparently, Gabrielle held Sloan responsible for her father's death. Victoria had estimated, based on comments Jordan had made to coworkers at the agency, that she believed her father to have been a great man. She'd spoken highly of him and her wistfulness related to his death had been apparent during those conversations. Of course she hadn't once mentioned his name. Now she was apparently out for revenge.

A.J. closed the folder and relaxed into the aircraft's luxurious leather seat a little more deeply. He found it difficult to understand how a parent could lie to their child, or neglect their offspring for that matter. By all accounts, Gabrielle fell smack into the category of the abused and neglected. That sort of childhood twisted a person's thinking. He could only imagine how it felt to have no one in the world to depend on. He wondered if that was the reason she'd worked so hard to be the absolute best she could be. She'd had no one to count on but herself.

Though his father had been a strong disciplinarian, A.J.'s formative years had included a secure and loving environment. He'd earned his hard knocks as a military man. He'd jumped in at age seventeen and then spent the next fifteen years proving what he was really made of. An injury and the life-threatening infection that followed during his time in Afghanistan had ended that career. He didn't talk about it. He shifted in his seat. Victoria was the only person at the agency who knew about it. His physical shortcoming prevented him from future military service, but it didn't stop him from being a damned good investigator.

Being chosen by Victoria Colby-Camp as one of only a few new hires was proof enough.

A.J. Braddock wasn't down for the count by a long shot. He still had some good years in front of him.

With his experience in the desolate mountains of Afghanistan, tracking one misguided young woman in Mexico would be a piece of cake. He would not fail in this mission. Victoria was counting on him. And he needed his work at the Colby Agency to give him something to look forward to, to hang on to. He wasn't ready to give up on being all he could be. No matter what the doctors said.

He wasn't dead *yet*.

Chapter Three

The Sierra Madre mountains, washed in green forest, jutted upward around the desolation of the desert and were a sharp contrast to all that surrounded it. The desert scrub and cacti of the expansive terrain she'd traveled for miles after leaving the village had given way to the rugged landscape at the foothills of the mountains, but the Jeep she'd rented had handled the drive easily.

Her patience and persistence had paid off. A kid, maybe twelve or thirteen, who'd made a delivery to the Sloan residence from the local market had given her directions.

For a price.

She hadn't haggled with him. At least, not once she'd seen a sort of kindred soul in his eyes. This kid hadn't needed any more grief in his life. From what Gabrielle had deciphered from the conversation, his mother was ill and he drove the broken-down truck his father had left behind when he'd deserted the family years ago. The kid helped put food on the table for his three brothers and sisters.

Life sucked that way all too often, Gabrielle decided. But the kid…he reminded her of herself. He wouldn't let it get him down. Instead he'd do what he had to. No matter the personal cost.

She focused a little more closely on the house in the distance. She'd decided that getting too close without sizing up the situation wouldn't be a smart move. Instead she'd driven around it, parked at the base of the mountains and then climbed for a while. Just long enough to find a decent position for scouting out the property.

"Some digs," she muttered as she surveyed the massive residence once more.

A fortress. A ten- or twelve-foot wall completely surrounded the property, which included a monstrosity of a house and sizable grounds, as well. A large iron gate allowed entrance from the front, if one possessed the proper credentials. Probably a numeric code at the very least. Another gate provided a secondary exit at the rear of the property. She could see a pool and what could be a detached garage or rather large workshop. The stuccoed exterior and red-tiled roof of the main house gave the place a rustic Southwestern style.

Apparently murder paid well.

Fury boiled up inside Gabrielle, but she wrestled

it aside. She had to stay focused. Losing her temper or having an emotional outburst would be detrimental to that task.

No vehicles were in view. She supposed they were parked in the garage. In the past half hour she hadn't noted any activity period.

Getting onto the grounds wouldn't be easy. She'd definitely have to wait for the cover of darkness to attempt any sort of move. Even then—she scanned the rear gate once more—security might include motion sensors. But that was a risk she'd just have to take.

Movement beyond the front of the property snagged her attention and she focused her binoculars to check out the vehicle approaching from the road that led to town.

Her heart rate bumped up a notch. This could be him. This could be Sloan.

The vehicle stopped at the gate. A truck. Full size. Maybe four-wheel drive judging by how high the chassis sat off the ground.

A man, dark hair, dark complexion, entered a code into the keypad. Not Sloan, Gabrielle decided. He had blondish hair and this guy looked like a native of the country versus just a guy with a deep tan.

As she watched, a woman in the passenger seat leaned past the driver and pressed her thumb to some part of the security keypad device.

Fingerprint analysis. Oh, yeah, Gabrielle had known security would be tight.

The gate opened and the truck rolled forward to park directly in front of the main entrance to the house. Before the two passengers were out of the vehicle, the gate had closed securely back into place.

If Gabrielle waited until the visitors left, she might be able to slip through the gate as it closed. It would be dark soon. She glanced at the setting sun. That might work. But she would need to get into position right away. Who knew how long these people would stay or whether or not they were permanent residents? They could be the hired help. The kid from the market had mentioned there was a man who helped around the house.

Gabrielle started to put her binoculars away and get to her feet, but new movement near the house stopped her.

What the hell?

She peered through the binoculars, hardly believing her eyes.

Two boys, one small, nine or ten maybe, another thirteen or older considering his manlike features, ran out of the house and toward the rear gate. Another man, this one much older and clearly Mexican with slight features, hurried after them.

The older man abruptly fell forward onto the stone courtyard. The driver of the truck rushed up to him. Shot the old man twice in the back.

Gabrielle jerked with each sound that echoed against the mountains around her. She scrambled to her feet, almost falling in the process.

"What the hell are they doing?"

The woman, the passenger from the truck, rushed up to the man with the gun. She appeared to be screaming at him. She, too, looked like a local. Dark hair, dark skin. Young.

The man with the gun grabbed her by the throat and said something to her. Something brutal, considering the cruel twist of his face. And then he ran after the boys.

Gabrielle tracked the course of the kids. They had made it through the rear gate but the man was gaining on them fast. Surely he wouldn't...

Her gaze swung back to the woman who was now kneeling next to the old man. The woman cried and rocked back and forth as if she'd just lost a loved one.

Gabrielle's attention shifted back to the kids. The older one was giving the guy with the gun a run for his money but the smaller boy...

"Damn."

The guy had the little kid.

Adrenaline seared through Gabrielle's veins. Her business here involved Sloan and only Sloan. Whatever the hell was going on with these kids was none of her concern. But she damn well couldn't stand here and watch some bastard hurt a kid. No way.

She tore out down the mountainside, careful to take the route she'd chosen on her ascent. The daylight was waning and she didn't want to risk falling.

By the time she'd reached her vehicle the man had rousted the two boys back through the rear gate, but he hadn't closed it. Cocky bastard.

Gabrielle jumped into the Jeep and drove as close to the house as she dared for fear of being heard. She bounded out of the vehicle and crept covertly onto the property.

Even before she'd edged up to the corner of the building she'd assumed might be a garage she heard the man with the gun ranting at his captives as well as his partner in crime.

"Tell me when your father will call!" he screamed, simultaneously ramming the muzzle of the weapon into the older boy's skull.

The boy told the man to go screw himself and Gabrielle couldn't resist a smile. "You tell him, kid," she muttered under her breath.

"Maybe I'll just kill you now, smart boy!" the killer warned.

"No!" the woman cried, only then moving away from the downed man. "You promised no one would die. What are you doing, Manuel? I don't understand!"

Gabrielle shook her head. Women could be so stupid when they were in love. She braced herself to take down the bastard with the gun.

She'd been training for a moment like this for weeks. She was the best in her class back at the firing range in *nowhere* Montana.

The sound of a weapon discharging exploded in the air.

Gabrielle's mouth dropped open and it was all she could do not to scream.

He'd killed her.

The man with the gun had shot his girlfriend.

He ordered the boys to get into his truck.

For ten, maybe twenty seconds, Gabrielle couldn't move. Her body felt paralyzed by what she'd seen. None of her training had adequately prepared her for this.

By the time she'd pulled it back together. the truck was driving out through the front gate.

She swore and rushed toward the two downed victims.

The man was dead for sure.

The woman gurgled and frantically flung one arm.

Damn.

Gabrielle surveyed the damage. The bullet hole in her abdomen was pouring blood. The one in her chest was a little too far to the right to have hit her heart, but maybe a lung. Gabrielle shook her head. How the hell did she know?

She needed help.

How did she get an ambulance way out here?

Her gaze zeroed in on the blood pooling on the ground around the woman's waist. Gabrielle swallowed hard. This girl wasn't going to make it.

Gabrielle pressed her left hand over the gut wound since it appeared to be the worst and tried to staunch the flow. "How do I call for help?" she asked the woman who still writhed desperately.

A dark brown gaze collided with Gabrielle's. "Stop…him…" The words were scarcely a breath of choking sound.

Gabrielle glanced toward the gate. "I don't…"

Icy fingers wrapped around her wrist with surprising strength. Gabrielle's gaze jerked back to the woman.

"I am…dying…" she gasped. "Help…the children." Her voice was barely audible now.

What did she do? Let the woman die or go after the children?

Gabrielle's heart pounded so fiercely she couldn't think.

"Take the…chi-children and hide…"

"What?" Hide? Panic tightened around Gabrielle's chest. What did she mean *hide?*

The woman's mouth worked but no words came out.

"Oh, God." Gabrielle lowered her head closer to the woman's face. Strained to make out her words. "I don't understand. What do you want me to do?"

"Hide…the children…more bad men will come…"

Gabrielle reared back at the warning. "Your friend isn't alone in this?"

"…many more will come…"

The woman stilled. Her eyes lost their desperate appeal.

Gabrielle's breath caught. She stared at the wounds that still oozed blood, but the force was much less now.

"Look, lady, I don't know—"

The woman remained completely, unnervingly still.

Gabrielle felt for a pulse. Nothing. Damn! She tried to get the woman's heart beating again, but it was no use.

The kids.

Dammit all to hell.

Gabrielle glanced at the gate, then back at the woman.

Someone had to save those kids.

There was no one but her.

Without taking a moment to second-guess herself, she bolted toward her Jeep.

If Sloan's residence was tied in with any kind of security monitoring system then maybe help was already on the way. It was too late for those two, but someone needed to know what had happened here.

One thing was certain, if Gabrielle was going to catch up with the son of a bitch who had the kids, she had to move fast. She jumped behind the wheel of her Jeep, wiped her bloody hands on a T-shirt lying on the passenger seat and twisted the key in the ignition.

The motor started and she released the clutch, allowing the vehicle to lurch forward. She sped out over the sandy landscape, dust flying behind her. But that was good because it was flying behind the other guy, too, and that was the only chance she had of keeping him in sight.

The sun had almost completely set, leaving only the thinnest purple hues reaching across the barren desert in front of her.

She couldn't turn on her headlights. She needed to get close enough to shoot out this jerk's tires before he noticed her approach.

She would figure out what to do next after that.

Chapter Four

Gabrielle slammed on the brakes.

The Jeep skidded to a halt and she bailed out.

Feet wide apart, she took aim. Her heart hammered against her sternum but she ignored it. She stared down the barrel of her 9 mm at the rear tire of the kidnapper's vehicle. Told herself she could do this. Her forefinger instinctively curled around the trigger.

The truck abruptly swerved and slid to a halt.

Gabrielle swore, adjusted her aim. Dammit, the truck was stopped with the passenger side facing in her direction. She could make out one of the kids....

The shooter registered in the corner of her eye a split second before she dove for the ground.

A series of explosions rent the air. Bullets plowed into the sand a few inches from her head.

She rolled. Took aim again.

A smile curled the corners of her mouth.

"Gotcha." She fired.

The man screamed and scrambled out of sight behind the vehicle.

"Dumb bastard."

A spray of bullets pelted the sand around her. She lunged for the cover of her Jeep. She'd been able to see some part of one leg beneath the truck. She'd hit him. Probably hurt like hell, but he wasn't dead by a long shot.

She studied the truck, except she couldn't see anything now. No movement whatsoever. "Damn." He had her at a distinct disadvantage. She couldn't shoot anywhere near the cab for fear of hitting one of the kids.

Where the hell was he?

He was still behind the truck…evidently using the tires for additional cover since she couldn't see any part of his lower anatomy beneath the vehicle chassis.

Gabrielle scanned the darkening landscape beyond the truck. Help didn't appear to be coming. Worse, the dying woman had said others would come. Friends of the jerk currently exchanging lead with her.

She couldn't just lay here and wait to see what happened. She had to make a move.

Screaming from inside the truck cab abruptly snagged her attention. What now?

She heard the shooter yell at the kids to shut up. Gabrielle's nerves jangled. If he started shooting at those kids…surely he wouldn't do that. He'd obviously had some reason for wanting to kidnap them, would likely need them alive for that purpose.

Gabrielle took a moment to find calm. Staying alive required slowing the blood roaring through her ears. It meant being aware of the other guy at all times and not letting her emotions take control.

The sound of wailing jerked her into forward motion. More arguing between the man and one of the boys. She had to try to reach the rear end of the truck while he was distracted.

Too late.

She didn't have to see the bullets pelting the sand, the echoing sound of the weapon firing was enough. He was laying down ground fire in an attempt to hit her or to force her away from her destination. She dove for the ground.

The truck horn blared to life. The gunshots stopped. Screaming and cursing followed.

Gabrielle scrambled to her feet and reached the side of the truck, hunkered by the tire to listen. The man still ranted at the older boy. Gabrielle decided the boy had laid down on the horn to distract the bastard or to annoy him. Either way, she'd have to thank him later.

Abrupt silence warned her that her enemy had figured out her latest move.

She held her breath. Listened…leaned down to see if there was any sign of his feet and legs.

Nothing.

He had to be crouched on the other side of the rear driver's side tire. Less than a dozen feet away.

The proverbial Mexican standoff. How ironic.

A thud had her fingers tightening on her weapon.

She listened intently.

Nothing.

She couldn't just continue to crouch here until he came around the end of the truck after her. But then he could be waiting for her to make exactly that kind of move. Evidently was.

Still no sound. No movement.

Damn. What the hell did she do now? Her mini weapons training course hadn't included anything like this.

She looked under the truck again. Couldn't see a damned thing.

Hovering here and waiting for him to come after her was driving her nuts. She had to move.

She eased quietly toward the end of the truck. Stalled there to listen.

Not a sound.

She peeked beneath the truck, but couldn't see a thing in the deepening gloom. Hell, he could be waiting for dark. The sun had already dropped behind the mountains, leaving only a faint glow reaching across the desert.

That thought propelled her into action. She moved around the end of the truck, to the far side of the tailgate. Steeled herself. Then risked a look beyond the corner…

The shooter was on the ground. Not moving.

Gabrielle frowned. She definitely hadn't gotten in a lethal hit.

His weapon was still in his hand, but he made no move to aim it toward her. Then she saw the reason for his motionlessness. Blood. Or what was likely blood. The sand around his lower body was dark with it.

Considering his eyes were still open and he hadn't blinked, she figured he was dead or damned close.

She darted to his position and kicked his gun away from his hand. He didn't move.

He'd been crouched near the tire as she had suspected. Looked as if he'd simply fallen over. Why had he bled so profusely?

She looked for the entry wound where she'd hit him, but it was difficult to see in the near darkness. Instead she looked for where the blood appeared to start on his clothing. Left thigh area.

Then she knew. There was an artery in that general area. She couldn't remember what it was called or exactly where it was, but apparently she'd hit it.

And he'd bled to death before he'd realized how badly he was wounded.

Damned lucky for her.

"Get us out of here!"

Her gaze swung to the truck and the older boy's face. He peered out the rear window now.

The two must have hunkered in the floor after the horn-blowing incident. Otherwise they could have seen the man lying on his side in the sand.

Gabrielle hurried to the driver's side door and wrenched it open.

"Hurry, lady!" the older boy demanded. "He was meeting his friends. They'll know something has gone wrong and head this way soon!"

"Give me a minute," Gabrielle snapped. Ungrateful kid. Didn't he realize she'd just saved his butt?

The boys' hands were chained together. The end of the chain was also bound to the bottom of the front seat. No way he'd reached that horn with his hand. He must have done it with his foot. The console between the front bucket seats would have allowed for a reach like that.

"I'll need the key," she said as she picked through the stuff in the console. The key in the ignition was alone on its ring. Shooting the chain to break it might work in the movies but she wasn't going to risk it under the circumstances.

"It's in his pocket," the older kid said. "Hurry!"

She rushed back to where the guy lay on the ground and crouched next to him. The gun had been in his right hand so that made him right-handed. The key would likely be in that pocket, which meant rolling him over.

Touching a dead guy ranked really low on her list of things to do in life. Unless it was Sloan, she amended. But the situation sorely limited her options.

Bracing one hand on his shoulder and the other on his hip, she rolled him onto his back. She shuddered but didn't hesitate to pilfer through his right pocket. Her fingers encountered cool metal and then curled around a single key. She tugged it out of his tattered jeans and rushed back to the truck without allowing her gaze to linger on the dead guy.

"Hurry!" the older boy shouted.

She scowled at him, her fingers poised on the lock. "I'm doing the best I can. You wanna give it a rest?"

He scowled right back at her. The ingrate.

The chains fell away and she ushered them out of the truck's back seat. "Get in my Jeep," she ordered.

The older boy, who was at least a couple inches taller than her, glared down at her. "Who are you? What are you doing here?"

Before she could answer, the little boy slammed against his brother's side and started to cry hard. He'd evidently gotten a look at the dead man on the ground and then launched himself at his older brother.

"Just shut up and let's get out of here," she snapped at the older boy who still glowered at her.

She stomped off in the direction of her Jeep. It wasn't necessary to turn around and make sure they were following. She knew they were. She could hear the younger boy's hiccuping sobs.

It was a shame the kid had to see the dead guy, but it couldn't be helped.

When they'd loaded into her Jeep, the smaller boy in the back seat, she and the older one up front, she started the engine.

"Better head for the mountains," the older one told her, his voice somewhat calmer now if not friendlier.

Gabrielle shoved the gearshift into first. "Why the mountains? Why not into town? To the police?"

Their gazes met across the narrow expanse of darkness that separated them in the Jeep's cramped interior. She didn't need to see his eyes well to recognize the intensity there, his voice told her all she needed to know.

"They'll be coming from that direction. You don't want to run into them. We need to hide. There's only once place we can go where they won't find us."

"The mountains, right?" she said, wondering vaguely how the hell she'd gotten caught up in this insanity.

"I know a place where we'll be safe. My father said if anything ever went wrong when he was away that we should go there."

She let off the clutch and the Jeep shot forward. "I hope you know the way." It wasn't as though she was from around here. She hated to break that newsflash to him, but there was no point beating around the bush. If more of those bastards were headed this way, they had to make a definite decision on which way they were going and the kid wasn't being exactly specific.

"I know the way," he said, a kind of resigned determination in his voice. "You just drop us off at the foot of the mountain and let me borrow your gun and we'll be fine."

Yeah, right. "I don't think so, pal." Did he think she

was stupid? She'd need this weapon to get back out of here. Maybe she should have taken the dead guy's gun for backup, but she hadn't thought of it until now.

"Then you can just drop us off and be on your way," he snarled, but his hateful tone fell a little short. His voice quavered ever so slightly.

"I can do that," she retorted, refusing to let the idea that he was probably scared to death get to her. The sooner they were out of her hair, the better she'd like it. She was no babysitter. She damned sure wasn't going to see after kids who most likely belonged to her enemy. Not that the kids deserved to be hurt because their father was a murdering lowlife, but it wasn't her place to do any more for them than she already had. She'd risked her life as it was.

The short journey was made in silence other than the soft sobbing in the back seat. The sound had lessened somewhat but not completely. Poor kid. He'd watched three people die today. It couldn't be easy on him.

She glanced at the older boy. She couldn't really see him that well with only the aid of the dim glow from the dash lights. His profile looked hard, his jaw determined. Instead of crying like his little brother, he'd opted to be angry. Not that she could blame him. She didn't know who the first man to die was or what relationship he had with the boys, but she'd guess a caregiver of some sort.

Irritation twisted inside her. Here she was getting all

worried about two kids who were no concern of hers. She had a goal to accomplish. She couldn't let anything get in her way. Not now. She was too close.

"Stop here."

She braked to a halt and resisted the impulse to ask for a please. Where were this kid's manners?

He opened his door and got out, then offered his hand to his brother. When the younger boy had climbed out, the older one hesitated before closing the passenger door.

"Thank you," he said. His lips trembled once before he bit them together, but she couldn't have missed it.

As tough as he wanted to appear, he was shaken up pretty badly, as she'd suspected.

"No problem." She looked out at the darkness. "You take care of yourselves now."

That was when she made her second mistake of the day. She turned back to the boy and this time it was his eyes that she zeroed in on. Blue eyes. Eyes so intense she couldn't look away for five or six seconds.

"We'll be fine," he assured her in that irreverent teenage tone.

She should have left it at that. But something in the kid's eyes wouldn't let her leave them.

"Maybe I'll just make sure you get where you're going." What the hell was wrong with her? Why did she say that?

"Suit yourself." The door slammed, practically in her

face, leaving her sitting there wondering why she wasn't driving away.

Because she was a fool.

Chapter Five

A.J. stayed out of the way as the local authorities took away the bodies of Pablo Vencino and a young woman whose identity was as yet unknown since no ID had been found on or near her body.

The truck he'd encountered on the road to the house had belonged to one Manuel Estes whose body had already been taken away.

A.J. was no coroner, but he estimated that the caliber of bullet used on each victim was the same—9 mm. Not to mention he'd found a few slugs in the sand near the abandoned truck. He hoped like hell Gabrielle hadn't made that kind of mistake.

The officer in charge had suggested that the murders had occurred during the night, perhaps twelve hours prior. A.J. agreed, taking into account the condition of the bodies. He had arrived at the airfield near Floresci-taf just after midnight. He'd come straight to Sloan's residence, coming upon the truck en route. After a thorough perusal of the residence, he'd telephoned the local authorities.

A telephone call to Victoria garnered no additional information. She hadn't been able to reach Sloan.

Neither A.J. nor Victoria was prepared to believe that Gabrielle had done this heinous thing, but both had to admit that the situation looked less and less favorable.

The sun rising over the mountains beyond Sloan's home cast a harsh, revealing light on the stone courtyard and the gruesome scene. A.J. shook his head. Whatever had happened here, if it involved Gabrielle, he had to ensure it didn't happen again.

The sound of a vehicle arriving at the front of the house registered briefly, but it wasn't until he heard the wail rent the air that A.J. realized company had arrived.

A woman, sixtyish, Hispanic, rushed to the gurney where Pablo Vencino's body lay. Two officers restrained her before she flung herself upon what was obviously her loved one.

"Señor Pablo's sister. Her name is Rosa."

A.J. turned to the man who stood at his side. The officer in charge, Detective Cervantes.

The woman's anguished cries resonated like a desperate musical score composed for just such an unholy scene.

She suddenly froze, a look of sheer horror claiming her face, evicting the agony. *"¿Donde estan los niños?"*

She looked from one of the officers restraining her to the other. *"¡Los niños! ¿Donde estan los niños?"*

"Is she referring to the children who live at this residence?" A.J.'s pulse started to pound. He and Victoria had assumed the children were with Sloan and his wife Rachel. But this woman, Rosa, was asking about the children. The image of the chains he'd seen in the back seat of Estes' truck abruptly thrust into his awareness. "Mark and Josh. Sloan's sons."

Cervantes gestured for the woman to be brought to him, then launched into a Spanish exchange that A.J. couldn't quite keep up with, mostly because of the woman's extreme emotional state and the detective's frantic pace of questioning. He did understand that Cervantes was attempting to verify the identities of the children the woman referred to, as well as the location of the parents, Trevor and Rachel Sloan.

Ten minutes later Cervantes had ascertained that Sloan and his wife were out of the country, at some hospital or medical clinic. The children had been left in Pablo's care. His sister had not seen him since Sunday, three days ago, but she had spoken with him early yesterday. All had been well at that time.

The questioning moved fairly smoothly until Cervantes asked about the woman who had been found with Pablo. Since her body had already been secured in a transport bag and placed in the waiting ambulance, Rosa hadn't known there was a second body.

When Cervantes described the young woman, Rosa's knees buckled and the officer on either side of her was all that kept her vertical.

The young woman turned out to be Rosa's niece, Valerie. Occasionally, Pablo permitted her to work at the Sloan residence, mainly when he needed additional help. Pablo had been a proud man and refused to admit he required assistance of any sort when it came to taking care of Mr. Sloan's home, the woman insisted through her tears.

The missing children put a whole new spin on the situation.

A.J. excused himself and moved back into the house to call Victoria again. As much as he wanted to go with the scenario that Gabrielle wasn't involved in these murders since her background indicated no such tendencies, he couldn't be certain. She might be far more desperate than he thought. That just didn't feel right. Wanting her revenge on Sloan was one thing, but killing innocent people, well, that was another. He just couldn't see it. But he fully understood that he might not be looking at the situation with optimal objectivity.

His call was put through to Victoria right away. It was scarcely daylight in Chicago and the agency was already up and running. Alert status, A.J. considered. He knew all about those situations.

"We have a new development," he said, not looking forward to passing along this new information.

The silence on the other end of the line telegraphed loudly how very much she did not want this to be worse news. Pablo's murder was bad enough.

"Has Sloan returned?"

Those three words carried enormous tension. Victoria comprehended better than anyone how this could end.

"No. It's the children. Apparently, Sloan and his wife are out of the country at a hospital or medical clinic for reasons we haven't learned as of yet. The children were left in Pablo's care."

More of that haunting silence.

"No other bodies have been found, so we have to assume the children have been taken by whoever killed Pablo," A.J. continued.

The ongoing silence pumped up the tension he already felt another notch or two.

"The priority of your assignment has just changed," Victoria said, her tone oddly flat. "Find those children, A.J., whatever you have to do I want them found ASAP."

"And Gabrielle?" His anticipation ratcheted up another notch as he waited for final clarification. He didn't want to have to mention Gabrielle to the local authorities. He knew all too well how it would go from there.

"She is still your assignment, but finding her is secondary to finding the children. As much as I don't want her and Sloan to run into each other, the children have priority now. No exceptions. Find them, A.J. I'll send

Amy Calhoun down to wait at the residence for Sloan to call or return. I want you focused entirely on the children."

"Done."

A.J. severed the connection and would have returned to the clean-up detail outside, but Cervantes entered the enormous kitchen just then.

"We need to discuss your participation in this case, Mr. Braddock," he said.

A.J. had already explained that he worked for the Colby Agency and that he was here to discuss a case with Sloan.

A.J. shrugged. "I don't know what else I can tell you, Detective. Sloan isn't here, so I won't be hanging around. However, since my boss is a close personal friend of Sloan's, she will be sending another investigator down to await his return."

Cervantes' gaze narrowed. "Why do you not wait, Mr. Braddock?"

A.J. dropped the phone back into his jacket pocket and retrieved a business card. "I have another assignment. I hope you'll keep the agency informed of the progress on the case."

"I may have questions," Cervantes countered.

A.J. tapped the card he held. "They will know where I am at all times if you need to reach me."

Still looking suspicious, the detective tucked the card into his pocket. "I will call."

The last sounded exactly like a threat, but A.J. let it pass. It had been a stressful morning for all involved.

Outside, one of the officers approached Cervantes and launched into a rapid-fire conversation with his boss. A.J. listened as best he could without being too obvious. Something new had been learned about Manuel Estes, the dead guy next to the truck.

When the lower-ranking officer had rushed off to pursue the lead, Cervantes turned to A.J. "Mr. Estes is apparently involved with a group of smugglers operating out of Mexico City."

"Drugs?" That was A.J.'s first thought.

Cervantes shook his head slowly from side to side. "White slavery." He shrugged. "Possibly this event was an effort to kidnap the children that failed on some level."

But not on the level that counted. The children were, indeed, missing.

"You'll keep my agency informed about this, as well?" A.J. asked, anxious to get out there on the trail of the children.

Cervantes agreed to do so, but still didn't appear happy to see A.J. leaving. That he didn't insist A.J. stay for further interrogation or observation said enough. Cervantes fully understood A.J. would be pursuing the investigation. He apparently didn't want to stop him. If A.J. could solve the case, that would save Cervantes a great deal of manpower and stress.

Worked for A.J.

A.J. climbed into the SUV that Victoria had arranged for him and drove back out to the truck. A.J. parked and got out. Whatever had happened with the children happened here. Estes had chained them together in the back seat and hauled them away from their home.

Had the group from Mexico City decided to take over the operation from here, cutting out the middleman? Or was this Gabrielle's work?

A.J. had no idea how long forensics would take down here. Until ballistics was complete on the shell casings found at the two scenes, there would be no way to know how many weapons were involved and which one killed Estes.

He walked the area around the truck, then surveyed the landscape beyond on all four sides. Where had the person or persons who'd ambushed Estes stopped initially?

That the desert wind had laid low last night and this morning worked to A.J.'s advantage. The sand was fairly undisturbed in places. As he moved cautiously around the truck he noted several sets of tracks. Some appeared smaller, less likely to belong to Estes or any other adult male. Two smaller sets drew him into a squat for a closer look. One set looked distinctly narrower than the other. Female, most likely.

Gabrielle.

A.J.'s jaw tightened. Near the driver's side door there appeared to be more than three sets of tracks, but it was difficult to distinguish one from the other between the numerous steps taken and the slight alterations made by occasional gusts of wind, however mild.

He hadn't been able to do this when he'd first arrived in the middle of the night. But now, with the sun beating down on the sand, he could make out a number of details.

Following the confusing cluster of tracks, he walked about twenty yards west of the parked truck. After long minutes of careful exploration he determined that this was where the entourage had taken an alternate form of transportation. The vehicle tracks, what he could make out, appeared to travel westward. Seemingly back toward the Sloan property.

A.J. drove around the massive compound and parked fifty or so yards from the rear gate.

Nearly an hour later A.J. had found where the vehicle continued its journey. His gaze tracked the general direction and concluded that the group had headed into the mountains. It didn't make sense, but the tracks didn't lie. Why would Gabrielle take that route?

He followed the most logical course and parked his SUV in a cluster of scraggly evergreens where the landscape started upward. Then he walked some more. Carefully considering every square foot of the ground he covered. Looking for anything not caused by nature. A broken limb, scattered rocks, anything.

Another hour passed before he found what he was looking for. A vehicle hidden much as he'd hidden his own.

Jeep. Engine was cold. He scanned the interior for any evidence of who had inhabited the space last.

Nothing. Except a T-shirt smeared with blood. Tension arced through him.

If this was Gabrielle's work, she was damned good at covering her tracks.

A smear on the back of the driver's seat captured his attention. He leaned in closer. Touched the stain. Deep, rusty red. Gritty texture.

Blood mixed with sand. The smear pattern suggested the sole of a sneaker. Same pattern he'd noted amid the confusion of tracks where individuals had exited the truck and then again where they had climbed aboard this Jeep.

Doing a mental comparison of the sole pattern in the blood smear and that of the similar one in the sand, he would say the shoe belonged to a child. Maybe the younger of the two boys. He had likely stepped in the bloody sand near Estes' body. There hadn't been any blood smears or stains inside the truck, assuming the children had left the residence in the truck. And that was the way this scenario was forming in his mind.

Estes had killed Pablo and his niece. He'd fled with the children and then was intercepted by someone.

Maybe Gabrielle. Maybe the bad guys from the smuggling operation for which he reportedly worked.

A.J. stared up at the rugged mountains. There was only one way to go from here.

GABRIELLE SAT stone-still as sunlight crept through the trees and underbrush, shielding her position. The morning was deadly quiet. But she didn't have to hear any sound to know she and the children were not alone in the woods.

She glanced at the two boys still huddled together and sleeping. The temperature had dropped considerably last night and huddling together had been the only way to stay warm. The older boy, Mark, she'd learned from the younger brother, had refused to lay near Gabrielle. Nature had taken over though after he'd fallen asleep. His body had instinctively sought warmth.

Her gaze strayed to the younger boy. Josh. His dark hair was the same as hers. Too much so, in fact. But it was his eyes that twisted her insides. Dark, dark, black eyes. Eyes she had never seen in person but would recognize anywhere.

Gabrielle hadn't noticed at first. She'd been too busy trying to rescue the two boys from their would-be kidnapper. Then she'd been occupied with putting some distance between them and the evidence of their escape. Staying alive had been top priority. Besides, it had been pretty much dark when the whole damned thing had gone down.

It wasn't until this morning that she'd gotten a look at the kid's eyes. He'd sat straight up and looked directly at her. His stare had lasted maybe ten seconds then he'd snuggled back up to his brother and gone back to sleep.

Gabrielle had sat there, stunned. She had only seen one picture of her father. Her mother had bragged that she'd stolen it from one of his numerous passports. Gabriel DiCassi had been an extraordinarily handsome man. Coal-black hair and eyes of the same dark, gleaming color.

Her mother had destroyed the picture when Gabrielle was sixteen to get back at her for going to the prom with a senior. But Gabrielle had never forgotten the lines and angles of her father's face. Above all else, his eyes had stood out in her mind.

Josh had those eyes.

The shape of his face. His nose. Every damned thing about him was like her father.

How was that possible?

Her mother had never mentioned a sibling. This couldn't be right. Besides, what would one of her father's children be doing with Trevor Sloan? Her gaze settled on Josh once more. Was this boy the reason her father was dead?

Emotion tightened in her throat.

The file from the Colby Agency had mentioned Rachel Larson and her son Josh, but there had been no information regarding the boy's father.

The painful emotion morphed into anger.

She would never know her father. Who he had really been. What he was like. Nothing.

All she really knew about him was the way he'd looked.

Like Josh.

Gabrielle had inherited her father's dark hair, but not his eyes. She'd gotten her mother's gray eyes. That hadn't bothered her until now.

She gritted her teeth and forced back the emotions. She would not let this distract her.

But then, if Josh were Gabriel DiCassi's son, surely Rachel Larson could tell Gabrielle about her father. But would any of it be the truth, or merely Rachel's version of the truth?

Just like Gabrielle's mother, everyone had their own idea about the truth.

Focus, she ordered.

There was no time to worry about anything else. She would take these kids to safety and then she would return to Sloan's house and wait for him. Josh had told her last night that his mommy and daddy had gone to a special hospital. Mark had told him to shut up, which was the end of any information on the whereabouts of Sloan.

After gaining some ground last night, she'd selected a scouting location and watched for the enemy to arrive. If the dying woman's warning was to be heeded, Gabrielle needed to know what she was up against. If she and the boys had gone directly to the village where

Mark insisted they would be safe, the enemy might have picked up their trail and followed.

Gabrielle had watched the SUV arrive, four men with flashlights had unloaded. They had inspected Manuel's truck and then moved on to the private residence of Sloan. Once they'd confirmed that the children were gone, they had left.

She'd been surprised. She'd expected them to attempt to find the children. That was what this was all about, right?

Maybe, maybe not. Whatever the bastards had in mind, she couldn't hang around to see. If they intended to follow, they would likely do so at dawn. Knowing that was likely the case, Gabrielle had spent three hours last night moving upward and away from the tiny mountain village.

Mark had argued. He'd wanted to go straight to safety. Gabrielle had decided that he wasn't really afraid for himself but he needed to keep his brother safe. Since she had the weapon they'd done things her way, settling in for the night at the location of her choosing.

She stood, surveyed the area. The gray mist that had accompanied dawn had dissipated entirely now. She listened for the slightest sound.

At this point they should start moving across, in a zigzagging course, and toward the location of the village. Mark claimed to know these mountains well, but she'd gotten the impression last night that he was pretty much lost. But he may have wanted her to believe that. Or he could have simply been tired.

She'd hardly slept at all for fear that he would take his brother and run. As exhausted as Josh had been, his brother would have had to carry him in any event. Thankfully Mark had gone to sleep and stayed that way.

She checked her weapon again, tucked it into her waistband at the small of her back. The hooded sweat-shirt she'd brought along in her Jeep was all that had kept her warm last night. It helped to conceal her weapon, as well. She might just wear it until the rising temperature forced her to peel it off. Her shoulder bag contained her binoculars, her cell phone with its dead battery, her doctored passport and money. That was pretty much all she'd brought with her. She'd flown from Chicago to El Paso under an alias. A former Texan, she'd known where to go for weapons. She'd bought the Jeep and driven to Mexico. She'd covered all the bases. But she hadn't been prepared for this.

They had no food or water, so reaching the village as quickly as possible would be the most desirable strategy. Going back to Sloan's house for supplies before making this journey hadn't felt like a smart move. Still didn't.

"We need to get moving."

Gabrielle whipped around to face the older of the two boys. She cursed herself for showing her surprise. She hated that he could sneak up on her like that.

"No kidding. I've been waiting on the two of you to finish your beauty rest."

He strode up to her, towered over her just because he could. "We should have gotten there last night. My brother was cold last night. He'll be hungry this morning."

Gabrielle refused to be baited by the ungrateful man-boy. "You know the reason we couldn't make a straight line for the village. Do you want the bad guys to catch up with you and your precious baby brother?"

She hadn't intended for the demand to come out so cruelly, but it had just the same. Too late to take it back now. She'd definitely hit a nerve. Mark's face reddened with fury. His blue eyes turned a couple of shades darker, but to his credit, he kept his mouth shut.

"We're leaving now, because it's the right time," she added before he could regain any momentum and initiate a rebuttal as to whose idea it was and who was in charge. "Carry your brother if you have to." With that order still ringing in the air, she did what she could to plump up the leaves where they'd flattened them down. She made sure nothing else stood out like a red flag to indicate someone had used the spot as a rustic Hilton.

"We're ready."

Her gaze swung to Mark's. His sleepy-eyed brother clung to his back. As Gabrielle watched, he yawned widely. "Where's Mommy?" he asked.

"Don't ask questions," Mark rasped. "Go back to sleep."

"I'm hungry."

"Let's get moving," Gabrielle said, hoping to head off the whole we-have-no-food discussion. She was hungry herself. Talking about it would only make it worse.

When they'd been walking for half an hour or so, she decided to attempt some conversation. Okay, maybe decided was a flat-out lie. She wanted…needed information. Stupid as it sounded, considering neither of these kids likely knew anything about her father. But they did know Sloan.

"Why did your folks have to go to a hospital?" That seemed safe enough territory.

"Mommy's having a baby," Josh piped up.

"Shut up," Mark snapped.

Gabrielle glared at him. "Stop yelling at him like that." She gave herself a good, swift mental kick for saying it so ferociously. He wasn't *her* brother. Not by a damned long shot.

Mark sulked for a while, then he answered the question. "She lost a baby a couple years ago. They're trying to make sure it doesn't happen again."

So Rachel was pregnant. Gabrielle couldn't help wondering how that child, or one of these would feel, if they never got to know their father.

Well, Josh hadn't. If her suspicions were on the money.

"That man back at the house," Gabrielle ventured, hoping the question wouldn't upset them further, "he was taking care of you?"

"He worked for my father. Took care of things," Mark said without explaining, but Gabrielle had pretty much decided the man had been a sort of butler or housekeeper.

"Pablo's dead," Josh said sadly. "So's Valerie."

So the kids did know the girl. "Did you know the man who hurt them?"

Mark glowered at her. "He didn't hurt them," he snapped, "he killed them."

Gabrielle didn't argue the point. He was right.

"Manuel was Valerie's boyfriend," Mark said eventually. "They'd stopped by once or twice before to help Pablo with things around the house. I don't think Pablo liked Manuel. He didn't trust him, for sure."

Well now they knew why.

"Why would Manuel want to take you and Josh?"

Mark shrugged. "Who knows? People disappear down here all the time."

That much was true. "Will someone at the village be able to reach your folks?"

Mark stopped abruptly. He faced her, his expression unyielding. "We can't bother them for this. If she gets upset, she might lose the baby. They can't know."

"She'll cry. A lot," Josh added knowingly.

Gabrielle didn't want to hear any of this. Whatever problems Rachel had were of no consequence. Gabrielle had her mission. She needed Trevor Sloan back here.

"What hospital did you say they were at?" she asked offhandedly as they started forward once more.

"I didn't."

Her gaze connected with Mark's and in that instant she saw the resolve there. No way was he going to endanger his father or his mother, or whatever Rachel was to him.

Gabrielle didn't have much choice, it seemed. She would ensure the boys reached the safety of the village and then she would go back and wait. Unless she could find something in the house that would tell her where Sloan was, she'd have no choice.

She put that out of her mind for the moment. Keeping all her senses on full alert was of primary importance.

Those men she'd seen last night would be hot on their trail this morning.

And if by some miracle they decided not to pursue the situation, that still left the Colby Agency.

Gabrielle knew without doubt that someone from the Colby Agency would be after her. The image of a tall, broad-shouldered man bullied its way into her head. She shivered. She told herself it was because she was still cold from sleeping on the ground last night. But that wasn't the case.

She banished the image and decided then and there that she didn't care who they sent after her.

The only question was whether or not whoever came was as good as Gabrielle or not.

Chapter Six

A.J. crouched and touched the earth. Cool. The three-some had been gone for an hour at least. He studied the area around the spot where he felt they had rested for a while during the hours before dawn. He couldn't help being impressed by Gabrielle's ability to disappear without having left much of a trail.

But she wasn't as good as him.

A.J. had twenty years' experience on her. He'd been tracking targets since he was a kid following his old man around the woods during hunting season.

He no longer doubted whether or not it was Gabrielle with the children. He knew it was.

She'd made her first mistake.

She hadn't policed up after herself where she'd rested during the night. He'd found three very long, very black hairs. Her hair. It wasn't much, but it was all he needed.

First rule of covert maneuvers: never leave anything behind for the enemy to find.

The question was, what the hell was she up to? Did she believe she could lure Sloan into some trap of her own making? And why would she kill a man to that end? Or was the man's murder an effort to rescue the children?

There wasn't any way to estimate the motivation for that move, he could only assume. A.J. felt relatively certain there had been more than one visitor to the scene of Estes' murder besides the local authorities. If Estes was supposed to have rendezvoused with his partners in crime, they may have come looking for him when he didn't show.

A.J. stood, glanced around the dense woods. Evergreens, pines and oaks soared up from the rugged terrain, in places effectively blocking out the sun entirely. The air smelled clean and fresh. The scene could have been ripped right from the pages of a picturesque calendar. But the serenity seemingly all around him was not to be trusted.

If, as Cervantes suggested, there were others involved, then, in all likelihood, A.J. wasn't the only one out here looking for the children…and whoever had taken them.

But, he had to be the one to find them first.

Careful of each step he took, he examined the thick undergrowth as well as the decaying foliage covering the ground of the occasional clearing for signs of disturbance. Tiny broken limbs, damaged leaves, any indentations in the softer areas of the terrain. And if he was really lucky, the occasional imprint of a shoe sole.

Anticipation revved as his instincts kicked in and his movements went on automatic. Every sensory perception was devoted to finding the next clue that would help him follow the path they had taken. He eased across the landscape with an efficiency of movement and without leaving a traceable trail. There was no time to waste. His search uncovered a small cave, there were likely dozens in these mountains, but there was no sign of Gabrielle and the children.

The near nonexistent trail she'd left behind headed upward and to the west, then downward as if Gabrielle and her companions were lost or couldn't decide which way they wanted to go. A.J. paused along a sharply angled bend in what could only be called a goat trail. That she would resort to following this path or any other obvious one surprised him. Giving her credit, she apparently had faith in her ability to keep the evidence of her passage to a minimum. Only a trained tracker would be able to keep up.

Realization had him shaking his head in admiration as well as irritation. She understood that someone would be tracking her so she took an extra measure of precaution. Like laying a decoy route.

Unsure how long he'd been following the wrong trail, he retraced his steps until he reached the place where the clues had first become somewhat more obvious. When he'd noted the slight change, he'd blamed the lapse on mounting fatigue. The children would be tired and hungry. But he should have known it wouldn't be as simple as that.

A.J. thought about the young woman he'd watched at the Colby Agency. She'd been quiet and attentive, but he'd sensed a raw kind of energy radiating from her. He had felt certain that was part of what had made her so undeniably attractive as a recruiting candidate. Gabrielle would be intense and focused, not to mention relentless.

Case in point, a deceptive maneuver any team leader would be proud of. He shook his head again, tried his level best not to let his professional respect for the woman expand further. It was bad enough his high personal regard for her wouldn't be hindered.

The rhythm of his heart accelerated and A.J. cursed himself for allowing the attraction to simmer. He'd felt it the moment he laid eyes on her, but he'd dismissed the chemistry as out of hand. He had more than ten years on her age wise and she was a colleague. He'd had no business going there. But those facts didn't change a thing as the days had gone by. Every day he went to the office and she was there, her very existence making him want to know her on a wholly unprofessional level.

He'd figured it would pass with time, but he'd been wrong. Not even the news that she'd fooled them all and that she was now a fugitive changed his relentless need to reach out to her, to know her better.

That kind of indulgence was a mistake professionally

and personally. Not only would he be crossing a hazard-ous line professionally, he knew that personally he couldn't make a long-term commitment of any sort. His future was too uncertain. Allowing anyone else to get caught up in that aspect of his reality was just plain wrong. He wouldn't do it. Not to Gabrielle. Not to anyone.

He hadn't allowed himself to become intimately involved in nearly two years. He wouldn't now. Not until he had more answers and only time would give those.

A.J. sucked in a deep breath and reassessed his prey's movements. When he'd located a secondary path, he resumed his journey upward toward the next ridge. He decided that she'd likely acquired the older boy's help in laying down that decoy trail. If the kid knew these mountains, they could move a fair distance apart and meet back up close to their ultimate destina-tion, but A.J. wasn't sure Gabrielle would want to let the kid out of her sight. Again, how she interacted with the children would be relative to whatever motive drove this escape into the mountains.

The destination couldn't be that far away, taking into account that they probably had no food or water. The trip hadn't been planned. Gabrielle was improvis-ing here, but doing a damn good job.

He cleared his mind of the thoughts related to her ability and refocused his full attention on staying on track. He felt reasonably certain he was closing in. Alone he could move faster than a woman and two kids. Even if he had temporarily gotten off course.

The crack of a twig made him freeze. He listened. Not Gabrielle, he decided, since the sound had come from well behind him. And his gut told him she wouldn't screw up so blatantly. Doubling back like that would cost her too much valuable time and without survival supplies that could be dangerous business.

Then again, maybe there was no ultimate destination. Maybe she was acting on instinct, operating by the seat-of-her-pants method. Also risky business.

If this wasn't Gabrielle, then someone else was either tailing him or following the same path he'd pursued this far. There were only two groups who could know he'd opted to take this journey into the woods. The local authorities because Cervantes likely had someone watching him as he'd left Sloan's residence and any cohorts Estes may have had. Estes' friends, if they still wanted the children, could be nearby. Either scenario wasn't particularly optimal. The cops tromping around up here could send his target rushing deeper into this craggy terrain. The latter possibility could cause far more trouble.

A.J. immersed himself into the underbrush like a sniper taking cover in preparation for long-term observation. He soundlessly pulled the foliage in around him and sat stone-still.

As he watched, three men emerged, with a surprising lack of noise considering their lumbering movements, into the area where Gabrielle had opted to put down a decoy situation. The men were Hispanic, late twenties to early thirties, and well armed.

Estes' friends, he surmised.

A.J. wondered again if Gabrielle had any idea just how much trouble she was in.

His tension didn't ease until the group had taken the bait and followed the wrong trail. A.J. would like to have been smug about it, but since he'd made the same mistake he decided it was better to be thankful for his training and leave it at that.

When enough time had passed, he surfaced from his hiding place and headed after his target. Reaching Gabrielle quickly was critical now.

A single second could mean the difference between life and death…possibly for her as well as the children.

THEY HAD company.

Gabrielle held very still and listened.

Following her cue, Mark and Josh did the same.

Her heart thudded in her chest but she ignored it, she had to determine exactly how close the enemy was.

Too damn close.

She turned to Mark. "How much farther to the village?" The words were scarcely a whisper, it was a miracle he heard her at all.

"Fifteen minutes."

That intensity that took her aback time and time again flashed in his pale blue eyes. He was afraid though he would die before he'd admit it. Josh waited beside him, his smaller hand grasped tightly in his older brother's.

Gabrielle moved in nose-to-nose with Mark. "Listen carefully to me, I want you to take Josh and move as fast as you can toward the village. Try not to make too much noise, but let speed be principal."

"How many of them are there?" Mark's square jaw hardened, giving his male features an even more grown-up look. She couldn't help admiring what a good-looking man he would ultimately be.

She shrugged. "Three or four."

He moved his head side to side. "You can't take all of them by yourself."

Foolish kid. He was going to get himself and his brother killed trying to play hero. "I said," she murmured fiercely, "take your brother and get the hell out of here, kid. I've got this under control."

"Mark, I'm really thirsty."

Their movements in concurrence, Gabrielle and Mark glared down at the boy. He blinked those dark eyes, the move doing nothing to conceal the absolute fear and exhaustion there. She was startled all over again when she stared into those too familiar eyes.

"Be quiet, Josh," Mark muttered. "It's okay. We'll get something to drink at the village."

"Take him, *now*," Gabrielle ordered. "We don't have

time to argue." As emphasis to her statement, she surveyed the wooded terrain around them. Standing here wasting time like this was dicey at best.

"Fine," he snapped a little louder than he should have. They both flinched. "Get yourself killed. See if I care."

And just like that he left, with his brother in tow and moving like a jackrabbit around nature's obstacles without making the slightest noise.

Gabrielle considered her options for a few seconds then made a decision. She would lead the enemy away from the direction the boys had gone. When she'd ensured they had made it to the village, she would return to Sloan's residence and wait for his arrival.

Then she would finish this.

She moved quickly, allowing her body to fight the terrain rather than flow with it. Broken sapling limbs and rustling foliage would be the result. If she were lucky, the bastards following her would think she'd gotten scared and clumsy.

Hesitating long enough to catch her breath, she listened above the sound of the air hissing in and out of her lungs and her heart bumping against her sternum. Nothing. Dammit. Where were they? Surely they hadn't picked up the boys' trail instead.

Maybe she'd have to drop back a few yards to see if she could determine the exact direction they'd taken.

When she would have turned to put thought into

action, a hand suddenly closed over her mouth. A powerful arm banded around her waist.

Fear rocketed through her veins. She kicked. Scratched at the hand clamped over her mouth.

"Be still," her captor snarled against her hair.

The gruff male voice sounded vaguely familiar but she didn't stop fighting him.

"Scream and we're both dead," he warned.

With that admonition still vibrating in her ear, he released her. She whipped around to face him, her weapon already in her hands and aimed right between his eyes.

A.J. Braddock.

For two beats she couldn't react. She'd known it might be him they sent…some part of her had hoped, but when faced with the man himself she felt abruptly overwhelmed.

"We need to take cover," he said quietly before glancing beyond her.

She snapped out of the trance she'd fallen into. No way was she about to fall for that one. She knew how that ancient trick worked. A quick peek over her shoulder and he'd take her weapon away from her while she was distracted. "I saw the movie, Braddock," she said smugly. "I'm not listening to anything you say much less falling for any of your tricks."

"Suit yourself." He cast around again as if visually trolling for trouble. "The guy you killed had friends. They're close."

"It was self-defense," she countered, a mixture of anger and fear—yes, dammit, fear, churned inside her. "I didn't set out to kill him."

"Save the excuses. We don't have time for them now."

He grabbed her and hauled her up against him. She bit her lips together to hold back a yelp as they went down into the sparse underbrush around a craggy out-cropping of rocks. The rocks, more so than the foliage, would provide some measure of cover. But not enough for her comfort if what he said was true.

"This isn't—"

He pressed a finger to his lips then pointed east of their position.

She followed his gesture and had to swallow a gasp.

Three men plundered through the woods like lumber-ing apes. She recognized the red shirt one of them wore. She'd seen these knuckleheads through her binoculars last night as she'd watched Manuel's truck and his dead body to see if anyone showed up looking for him.

They had picked up her trail and come for the children.

A new rush of fear spiraled through her.

Then she realized that the idiots were headed in the wrong direction. They'd taken the bait she'd left by way of a decoy path that would lead them right back to where they'd started...in about forty-five minutes, buying her plenty of time to do whatever necessary.

Before she could pat herself on the back, she remem-bered that another enemy hadn't fallen for her decoy.

That she was currently tucked against his unyielding body, her backside to his front, abruptly filtered into focus. He'd banded one of those strong arms around her middle again, ensuring she wouldn't be going anywhere until he decided she should.

Long minutes after the men had slipped out of visual range, Braddock still held her tightly against him. She'd managed, to that point, to block the feel of his muscular contours, but her defenses were failing her now. Her body had started to respond to the blatant maleness of his.

Not good.

"Let me go," she ordered under her breath.

He snatched the weapon out of her hand before she had the good sense to consider he might do just that.

"Just don't try anything we'll both regret," he advised.

She scrambled away from him, still conscious of the other enemy not so far away.

Braddock got to his feet with a little more grace. He towered over her by at least six inches, which made her all the more furious. Guys liked using their vertical advantage for an intimidation tactic.

"Where are the boys?"

There was something about the way he looked at her when he asked the question…something she couldn't quite label. And then it hit her.

"You think I did something to those kids?" Hell, she'd saved their lives. Didn't anyone care?

"That's—"

"Drop your weapon."

A.J. froze. He couldn't believe he'd let his guard down this way. He cursed himself repeatedly as he considered his limited options.

"What the hell are you doing?"

A.J. frowned as Gabrielle stormed over to him, past him actually. The pressure on the back of his skull eased and A.J. pivoted to see what the hell was going on.

Two young boys, Sloan's boys, huddled with Gabrielle behind him. The only weapon the older one had in his hand was a small pocket-size flashlight.

"Who is this guy?" the older boy demanded with a dark look in A.J.'s direction.

Deciding he could mentally berate himself later for being a complete fool, A.J. ignored the kid and snagged Gabrielle by the arm. "We have to get out of here. These kids are in grave danger."

She glowered at him. "Don't touch me."

"You heard her," the older boy said, his fists clenched for battle.

"You gotta be kidding," A.J. muttered under his breath.

The younger kid held on to his brother's wrist and stared wide-eyed at A.J.

Perfect.

He'd come here to rescue these boys and this was the thanks he got.

"We have to get moving," he reminded the woman who appeared just as startled by the boy's defensive stance as he did.

"He's not important," she said to the boys, "but he's right, we do have to get out of here."

A.J. didn't feel any compunction to thank her for clearing up that question.

She went on, "There are three men on our tail and they're close. We need to get you two to that village."

The older boy nodded his understanding. "Follow me."

"What village?" A.J. asked as he fell into stride with Gabrielle. If she thought he was going to let her continue to be in charge, she was crazy. First, he needed to know what the hell she was up to, then he needed to understand what this village had to do with the plan to get the children to safety.

"I don't know," she said without sparing him a glance. "Some place they've been taught to go when they feel they're in danger."

Well that answered that question without telling him anything at all.

A.J. kept an eye on their backs as the boys moved swiftly, expertly, along a crooked, rocky trail flanked by lush greenery that was, according to Mark, the older kid, a shortcut. He'd only taken it once and hoped he wouldn't get lost.

Just what A.J. had wanted to hear. At least it was taking them away from the direction the enemy had taken.

His gaze rested on the woman laboring to keep up with the teenager. She had to be exhausted, but she didn't slow down. Did she really have these kids' best interest at heart? Or was this move part of her plan to lure in Sloan?

He didn't know.

But he wouldn't let her out of his sight for a second. When the kids were delivered to safety, he would escort her back to Chicago. Amy Calhoun would take care of informing Sloan about what had happened. Mission complete.

Until then he'd just have to deal with the way the rhythm of his heart was disrupted every time he allowed his gaze to settle on her for more than a few seconds.

Fourteen minutes later and a final twisting turn in the trail led them into a clearing. That clearing rambled onward and sprawled amid the towering evergreens and oaks as if they'd backed out of the way to make room. Mud huts and rustic cabins spread outward from a center hub of a gathering place like the spokes on a wheel.

Heads poked out of partially opened doors but none of the residents appeared glad to see them. Certainly none rushed out to greet them.

Just when A.J. decided they were in the wrong place if an invitation to come in and stay awhile was expected, three people, two men and a woman, approached them.

Mark rushed over and allowed the elderly woman to hug him. Josh followed suit. A lengthy discussion in a language A.J. didn't understand ensued.

Not Spanish. Some primitive native language, he estimated.

Mark walked back to where A.J. and Gabrielle waited.

"We'll be safe here. Señor Camilo will take us farther into the mountains to a place where they go when danger threatens."

Gabrielle nodded. "Good." She glanced at A.J. "I guess we'll be on our way then."

Mark shot him a look. "You'll need water."

"Make it fast," A.J. warned. "The longer we're here, the more likely we are to draw attention to your position."

Mark double-timed it back over to the greeting committee and spoke briefly with the old man who appeared to be in charge.

The old man shouted toward one of the huts and in less than a minute a young man, about the same age as Mark but dressed in pants that looked too short and a cut-off T-shirt, trotted out with a container of water.

Mark brought the water to Gabrielle. The container looked to be made from animal hide with an attached strap that would allow for hanging over the neck and shoulder.

"Thank you," the boy said to her.

She took a long sip from the water, then wiped her mouth. A.J. followed the move with far too much interest.

"No problem," she told the kid.

A.J. felt his patience thinning. They needed to be on

their way. So did the villagers and these kids. They didn't have time for drawn-out farewells.

"Let's go," she said before he could.

He resisted the urge to toss back something inane like *'bout time*. He didn't know why it bugged the hell out of him that she'd bonded so quickly with a stranger. Male at that. And a kid, he reminded himself. Though he hadn't actually looked like a kid. Fourteen or fifteen maybe. Tall, well-muscled frame.

Enough, Braddock. He outright refused to label the emotion nagging at him. In his adult life, no one had ever caused him to lose his bearing so fully.

"Am I leading the way?" she asked, "or are you?"

He paused. Tossed her an annoyed glare. "I am." He started forward again, didn't look back. He didn't let himself dwell on just how low his cognitive level had dropped within minutes of finding himself in her presence.

They descended the rocky trail for about ten minutes before she spoke again. Yet he'd been keenly aware of her presence every single step of the way.

"So are you turning me over to the police? I only shot at that guy to keep him from hurting those kids. I didn't mean to kill him. It was an accident as well as self-defense."

Considering she'd already spent eighteen months in prison, he doubted she looked forward to a return trip.

"Nope. I figure you did this country a favor."

She hastened her step to stay even with him. "Then where are you taking me? Back to the Colby Agency?"

He stopped, leveled his gaze on hers though he fully understood he would likely regret it. "Yes. And you're not going to give me any trouble. You made a mistake, you have to make it right before you do something truly stupid."

The pouch of water she'd held close to her chest ever since the kid gave it to her suddenly flopped off her shoulder. His gaze followed the drop then abruptly jerked back up to find the snub nose of a .38 staring him in the face.

"No offense, Braddock, but I have other plans."

Damn. He was going to have to do this the hard way.

"Does that kid who slipped you the weapon know you came here to kill his father?"

She flinched but didn't waiver as he'd hoped she would.

"Guess not," he allowed, with a knowing look at the weapon.

"I'm not going back until this is done."

The determination in her tone told him she'd made up her mind and nothing short of death was going to change it.

"Do you really believe you can take on a guy like Trevor Sloan?" When she didn't answer, he added, "You won't survive the encounter, Gabrielle. You need to cut your losses and while you're at it, you need to get the real story on what happened between him and your father."

Now that appeared to give her pause.

"Don't even pretend you know what you're talking about, Braddock," she returned. "You don't know anything about this except what Victoria told you."

"And you only know what your alcoholic mother told you."

He hated himself for saying it even before the words were fully out of his mouth. The glimmer of hurt he saw in those gray eyes told him he'd gone too far. But the pain was immediately replaced with fury.

"Give me the weapons, yours and mine," she ordered.

"You're making a mistake, Gabrielle." He tried again. "Wake up before it's too late."

A disgruntled voice in the distance had both of them wheeling in that direction.

Gabrielle hissed a curse.

The sounds of the three men thrashing around in the underbrush told A.J. they were headed straight for their position.

"We'll have to divert them," he suggested quietly, palming his weapon. "We don't need them wandering any closer to the village."

"You're right, we have to head them off."

Surprised at her ready agreement, his gaze locked with hers.

"Then we'll finish this," she added.

"Then we'll finish it," he agreed.

With that settled, she grabbed the water and they ran like hell, making enough noise to attract the hearing impaired.

Chapter Seven

Bullets whipped through the trees, tearing bark from the trunks and splitting the leaves of underbrush.

Gabrielle ran like hell. She didn't dare glance behind her. Wasn't sure exactly where Braddock was. He was a big guy, he could take care of himself. And right now, it was pretty much every man for him or herself.

Waist-high bushes dragged down her speed. The higher undercanopy of smaller trees slapped at her face and blocked her view. Still she didn't slow down.

The occasional shout from one of her pursuers told her they were nowhere near ready to give up.

Damn.

The only thing she could do was keep moving.

"This way!"

She almost stumbled as Braddock rushed across her path.

What the hell was he doing?

No time to figure it out. She ran after him. Wherever

he was headed he sure seemed to have some destination in mind. That was more than she had.

A hand abruptly grabbed her by the arm and jerked her to the right. She slammed against Braddock's hard body. He stumbled back several steps, taking her with him. Darkness totally engulfed them both.

Gabrielle's chest seized as she sucked in a lungful of dank, musty air.

Cave.

As her eyes adjusted, she could see the opening where Braddock had waited for her to pass. One quick snatch and they basically tumbled in together. Thankfully the bushes and saplings crowding around the entrance pretty much blocked it from view.

"How did you find this place?" She kept her voice low, a fierce whisper. Mainly it ticked her off that he'd been the one to save their skin.

"I noticed it this morning when I was fishing for your trail."

"Lucky for us," she muttered. She shouldn't be surprised at his resourcefulness. He'd spent half a lifetime in the Marines. He'd probably done this a lot.

"I thought so."

Gabrielle froze at the sound of rustling foliage. They were close now. At least two of them. She bit down on her lower lip as the racket grew louder. What if they noticed the cave and looked inside? Would the enemy be able to see them in the darkness? The bastards might not notice Braddock since he wore dark clothing. Jeans, tee and button-down shirt all were navy. Even his fancy hiking boots were dark.

She, on the other hand, wore khaki pants that were stained with bloody handprints where she'd attempted to help the woman. The white tee and gray hooded sweatshirt didn't exactly blend in with the current environment, but then she hadn't expected to be running for her life in the mountains of Mexico.

One of the men shouted to the other that the area was clear. His voice sounded as if he were right outside their hiding place. Gabrielle shivered. She couldn't help it. Braddock's arms tightened around her and she shivered again, this time it wasn't about fear. Damn him. She didn't like that he could make her do that. But then, she had to admit, that she could get used to the feel of him snuggled up against her really fast.

She shifted to put some space between them.

His arms loosened with her movement but he didn't let go. Was he afraid she'd make a run for it? No way. Better the enemy she knew than the one she didn't.

The thought pinged her conscience. Braddock was her enemy, technically. She had to remember that, couldn't afford to let her guard down with him no matter how badly she wanted to.

Silence settled as the commotion outside the cave faded.

Long minutes passed and Braddock gave no indication that he wanted to get moving. Gabrielle worked at controlling her breathing and the shaky sensation that being this close to him in the dark had obviously set off.

It was totally stupid, but she couldn't stop the reaction. Maybe it was fatigue. She was tired. She'd hardly had any sleep and hadn't eaten in twenty-four hours. As hard and as often as she worked out, her typical routine didn't come close to paralleling the physical rigors she'd endured since rescuing those kids.

A frown wrinkled her forehead, punctuated the headache she'd tried to ignore for the last hour. How had she ended up rescuing Sloan's kids? Well, one of them was his anyway. She imagined that he considered the younger one his own, as well. The memory of those dark eyes nagged at her still. She felt certain Josh was her biological half-brother. Another piece of the past she hadn't known about.

"We need to make a decision."

She jumped at the sound of his voice though he spoke softly. Maybe it was just the reminder of how close he was. Right behind her.

"What kind of decision?" If he expected her to just give up and forget about settling her score with Sloan, he could forget it. She hadn't come this far to walk away.

"Whether or not we're going to attempt to walk out of here now or wait until dark."

The sound of his voice whispering over her skin made her tremble again.

"Are you all right?"

She jerked away from him. "I'm fine. I'm hungry, that's all." It was true.

He scrubbed his hand over his jaw. She didn't have to see the action, though she could make out some details now, she heard the rasp as his palm slid over the stubble on his jaw. More of those goose bumps tripped one over the other on her skin.

"I think it would be best if we stayed put until dark." Before she could protest, he added, "But I'll see what I can scrounge up in the way of eatables."

She rolled her eyes. Great. Mr. Survival was going to capture dinner and bring it back to the cave.

"I guess you're the boss," she muttered since he apparently waited for her to make some sort of response. On second thought, she amended, "for now."

"Stay out of sight. And whatever you do, don't go anywhere. We can't risk running into those guys in the daylight. We'll make plans when I get back. I won't be long."

Gabrielle hugged her arms around herself. God she hated the way this cave smelled. She shuddered at the idea of what sort of critters were likely hanging out in the dark with her. Staying in here any longer than necessary wasn't exactly appealing, but it beat the hell out of getting shot.

What was she doing letting him make all the decisions?

She should just get out of here before he came back. That way she wouldn't have to do anything she knew she would regret. She liked Braddock. Shooting him wasn't something she looked forward to.

Since he might not feel the same way, her best bet was not to put him to the test.

A.J. STAYED LOW, keeping his head below the level of the underbrush. He had no desire to play the part of bobbing duck in a shooting gallery.

No sign of the enemy.

As he'd tracked Gabrielle today he'd noticed a number of plants he recognized, several were edible. The wild strawberries and potatoes were the best. If he couldn't locate either of those, he'd settle for the tubular roots of golden grass. Not nearly as tasty, but readily available.

While he was out he wanted to attempt to get a fix on where the enemy had gotten to. He wasn't fool enough to believe they would give up this easily. And even if they seemingly did, they would likely watch his SUV and Gabrielle's Jeep. Walking back to Florescitaf or in the direction of Chihuahua wasn't something A.J. wanted to do. Transportation would be preferable.

Though he'd done so earlier today, he checked his cell phone again. No service. Not that he'd really expected any, but he could hope.

After following the tracks the scumbags had left, he

decided they'd headed back down the mountains. Probably hoped to head him and Gabrielle off before they reached their vehicles.

A.J. surveyed the jagged topography. If he knew the area better he might attempt another way out of here. But he didn't. The possibility of running into serious trouble with no supplies to lay low for the long haul would be suicide. Berries and roots would only go so far.

When he'd gathered what he could find without venturing too far, he headed back to the cave. It would be dark in an hour, maybe less. Even if the men had the vehicles covered, he and Gabrielle could attempt to reach Sloan's residence by foot. But if Sloan had returned home, that might not be the best move. Amy should be in place by now. If they reached the base of the mountain, cell service should be available and then he could give Amy a call and get the status of the situation.

Satisfied with his plan of action, he entered the cave slowly, giving his eyes time to adjust to the extreme darkness.

A.J. stopped. Listened. Allowed the sensations inside the cave to wash over him. The darkness, the moldy air, the emptiness. He didn't have to wait for his eyes to adjust to the lack of light.

She was gone.

He sighed. Maybe on some level he'd known she

would make a run for it. Maybe he'd even wanted her to…if her plan was to get the hell out of Mexico.

But she wouldn't do that. She had a score to settle and he wasn't going anywhere until she did.

He was going soft. There was no other explanation.

He'd let his personal feelings override his good sense. She'd saved the lives of those children. That was supposed to count for something, but it wasn't supposed to make him go stupid.

Back to square one. He encountered the water bag she'd left and dropped his bounty next to it, then headed out to correct his mistake. He would find her and he would take her back. And this time she wouldn't make him second-guess the rightness of his assignment. He didn't analyze why she'd left the water for him.

"Did you find dinner?"

She sauntered into the cave as if she hadn't done exactly what he told her not to.

"I told you to stay put." It was all he could do not to grab her and shake her. Didn't she understand how dangerous their situation was? Or was she just so reckless she didn't care? Maybe she had a death wish but he didn't.

At least he wasn't going to have to hunt her down again.

"I never was very good at following orders," she said blithely. "Just ask the guards at my last place of residence."

She walked around him and he pivoted to follow her movements as best he could in the near darkness.

"What is this stuff?"

She crouched and scooped up a handful of the goods he'd gathered.

"Consider it a salad without the dressing." He moved closer, dropped into a squat to help her sort through the offerings. "Wild potatoes. A few wild strawberries and roots. The roots could be exotic carrots."

She crunched into a potato. "Tastes like dirt," she commented between chews.

"A little dirt never hurt anyone."

"Just so you know," she told him before taking another bite, "I'm only eating this because I'm famished. If it makes me sick, you're in trouble."

A smile tugged at one corner of his mouth. "It won't make you sick." He ate slowly, careful to chew well. Not bad in a pinch, he decided. Like Gabrielle, he could have done without the dirt, but they couldn't afford to waste the water to wash the food. He didn't doubt there would be springs around here that offered good drinking water, though he couldn't be sure if they would stumble upon one.

As if reading his thoughts she said, "Would you like some water?"

"After you."

She took a sip, licked her lips. "This is why I came back." She passed the water pouch to him.

"For dinner?" He knew that wasn't what she meant but he didn't want her to know that.

"I didn't want to leave you out here without water. Then again I didn't want to go thirsty myself."

There was a sincerity in her tone that affected him far more deeply than it should have. Especially since it wasn't as though he was lost in the desert. He could be back at Sloan's property in two or three hours unless the enemy drove him deeper into the mountains.

He drank, careful to remember rationing was a good idea if not absolutely necessary at this moment, then passed the water back to her. Settling onto the ground, he decided to take a stab at getting the truth from her. "What's the real reason you came back?"

A moment of awkward silence throbbed between them before she relaxed into a sitting position. She exhaled a heavy breath. "One of the men is hanging out on the ridge about fifty yards from here. He was using binoculars to scan the landscape."

"They've split up," A.J. assessed out loud. "Two went south, probably spread out from there."

Another round of loaded silence told him she was still holding out on him.

"You understand that getting through this is largely dependent on our working together."

Another of those deep sighs.

"I really wasn't worried about the guy on the ridge," she admitted. "I could have gotten around him. But I overheard a call he made. He had a walkie-talkie. I could hear both sides of the conversation, not that he was taking any pains to keep it quiet."

A.J. didn't push, just let her talk. He had a feeling that she'd been pushed around far too much in the past.

"Whoever he reported to said he was sending in eight more men. They don't want us to leave this mountain alive, Braddock. And even though I couldn't understand every little thing that was said, it was more than clear that they want the children real bad. I don't think this is about white slavery or some random act of kidnapping. This is specific. This is about Sloan."

If half a dozen or more men were coming, it would be impossible for Gabrielle and him to take them all on. A.J. wasn't worried about getting caught and giving away the location of the children. He could handle any kind of interrogation techniques they tossed his way. He'd had training in every imaginable anti-interrogation technique. But the same couldn't be said for Gabrielle.

If she were captured, she would be a liability to the children's safety.

She ran her fingers through her hair. "I'm going to tell you straight up, Braddock, I don't give a damn about Sloan. In fact, I came here to put a bullet in his head or die trying. That goal hasn't changed." She fell silent again, as if she needed to compose herself before she said the rest. It was too dark now for him to read her expression with any accuracy.

"But those kids," she went on, "they didn't ask for any of this. They aren't guilty because of who and what their father is or has done. My—" Her breath caught and then he knew how difficult saying all this was for her.

He slid closer, reached out and rested his hand against her arm. "I know your childhood wasn't easy," he said softly. "You don't have to explain."

For the first time in her life Gabrielle wanted to believe the words she heard. She wanted him to hold her and to promise her that this would all work out. But how could she trust him? She'd never been able to trust anyone. Not even her own mother. How the hell could she trust this guy?

She cleared her throat and forced herself to say the rest. "She didn't protect me." Her fists clenched at the memory of how she'd barely escaped rape twice when her mother would pass out and leave one of her numerous boyfriends still wanting. But that was only part of it. Gabrielle took all the flack from impatient landlords and cops who wanted to take her mother to jail for public drunkenness or for writing a bad check. It was always Gabrielle who'd had to make everything right. She'd started handling adult problems when she was ten. It hadn't been fair.

"No one protected me," she reiterated. "I'm not about to walk away and let those sorry bastards use those kids for pawns or worse to get at their scumbag father."

Struggling for calm, she forced back the unpleasant memories. Right now was not the time to lose it like this. Her life was what it was. It could have been worse. She didn't go around feeling sorry for herself because her mother and father hadn't been there for her. But her experiences did make her keenly aware of situations like the one Mark and Josh found themselves in just now. Keeping them safe had moved into top priority on her list of things to do in Mexico.

A.J. watched her wrestle with her emotions. It wasn't so much what he could see in the near total darkness, it was what he could feel. She needed someone to believe in her. She needed to do this for those boys. But a part of her battled with that decision. The part, he surmised, that wanted—needed—revenge.

Considering that inner turmoil, now was not the time to go into who and what her father had been. Her emotions were far too raw.

"This changes things considerably," he admitted. Protecting the children was priority one. To that end they couldn't risk being caught, which meant they had to stay on the run and keep their hunters guessing. Eventually they would give up. Arriving at that point would damn sure be a lot easier if he and Gabrielle were prepared. Food and water were essential.

"I need time to think," he said. "We should stay here

for the night. They won't come back here looking for us. That stroke of luck will buy us a little time to rest and regroup."

"I don't have a better plan," she admitted. "But we can't stay here forever."

He wouldn't argue that.

"Why don't you try to get some sleep first? I'll wake you if there are any developments."

"You have any idea what sort of insects or animals might be in here?" She hugged her arms around her knees.

"The usual I suppose." Being too specific wouldn't help. Besides, whatever life forms this cave supported apparently didn't care for humans since he hadn't noticed anything attempting to latch on or creep in next to his skin.

Gabrielle wondered if that answer was supposed to give her comfort. "Thanks, Braddock, that was helpful."

She rested her head against her knees and tried to put the idea of insects or worse out of her head. Sleep was necessary to optimal physical performance. Being able to run like hell if need be was necessary to survival.

Her lips felt dry and there was still grit in her mouth from the dinner Braddock had scrounged up. At least her tummy had stopping rumbling.

To her surprise sleep started to drag at her. She wondered vaguely as she drifted off what he thought of her. It was a dumb thought. She knew the deal. A.J.

Braddock was the kind of man who could make a woman believe in fairy tales. And she, Gabrielle Jordan, knew without question that fairy tales did not, in any form or fashion, exist.

True love was a myth. One made up by desperate women who remained ever hopeful when cynicism would serve them better.

She was smarter than that. No man would hold that kind of power over her. She would keep it clean, un-cluttered. When she needed a physical fix it would be about sex, not love.

Six months, some wicked brain cell reminded. Six long months since she'd had sex. And that lackluster en-counter had been about needing to make sure she was still alive after eighteen months in prison. She hadn't wanted to be with anyone since.

Until now.

But A.J. Braddock was not a good candidate for a roll in the hay. He wasn't the type.

The last thing she remembered before drifting off was making a mental list of all the things he was... like caring....

BRADDOCK FELT CERTAIN she'd finally given in to the ex-haustion. She'd stopped shifting her position and her respiration had evened out.

He leaned back against the cool rock wall and tried to relax. He couldn't risk going to sleep but he did need to ensure his body rested. The weakness he felt was likely more related to the day's exertion than anything else. But he couldn't be certain.

His eyes closed and he let the memories come flooding back. He rarely allowed that anymore. But right now he needed to remind himself of what was real and what wasn't.

Permitting this attraction to loom further into dicey territory would be a monumental mistake. His future was too uncertain to rely upon, much less allow anyone else to.

He remembered the day, even the hour it happened. He'd cornered the enemy. It was the last day he would spend in Afghanistan, but he didn't know that then.

They'd raided a lab where experimental drugs were being developed. The setup was far too advanced to be an Afghani operation. It hadn't taken long to figure out it was just another attempt by international terrorists to create a virus that would wipe out the intended target: Americans.

He hadn't known that the enemy he'd cornered was infected. The man had fought wildly yet he was unarmed. Unable to bring himself to shoot an unarmed man, A.J. had battled him hand-to-hand and he'd conquered him. But not without injury. The fool had bitten him. Symptoms had emerged within twenty-four hours.

He hadn't been able to eat or sleep. Concentration had failed and then came the hallucinations. After weeks of enduring those debilitating side effects of the virus, the pain started. Fierce, unrelenting, accompanied by general malaise.

Eventually the symptoms had disappeared. A.J. had thought he was well, but additional blood work had shown the virus still present in his system. Additional research had discovered that the virus was not contagious beyond seventy-two hours. Just his luck that the guy who'd bit him had only been exposed forty-eight hours earlier. The only up side was that, like lupus or some forms of cancer, the virus would go into remission. He'd only had one relapse in the past two years, which had prompted him to get on with his life.

He could either sit around waiting for another relapse or he could live his life and take sick leave like any other working man when illness struck.

Unfortunately the end result was not known, which was the downside. The virus was inactive, but that could change at any time, constituting a constant threat to his immune system. Whether or not he would live out a normal life span was unknown. Truth was, not much at all was known.

Only that there was nothing anyone could do to stop it. He was totally at the virus's mercy. When it struck, he'd be bedridden for the duration.

Whether or not he could pass it on to offspring was unknown. Every test indicated sexual activity was safe, but he refrained just the same.

It wouldn't be fair to risk another person's health or heart.

His gaze instantly sought Gabrielle's sleeping form in the darkness.

No way would he introduce that kind of pain into her life. She'd had more than her share already.

What he could do was try to get her out of this alive and do his best to convince her that Sloan wasn't her enemy. That her father wasn't the man she'd been raised to believe he was.

A big job any way he looked at it.

But someone had to do it. She deserved to have a chance at a real life without all the baggage from the past.

The chance that someone else would be willing to look past all that attitude and sass was slim at best. He was her best shot at happily-ever-after.

Ironic, he mused. He was the last damned man on earth who had anything to offer and yet he was the only one who understood what she needed.

Trust. Acceptance. Understanding.

Chapter Eight

Gabrielle jerked awake. Her heart pounded so hard she could scarcely catch her breath. Her skin felt clammy and cold.

Where the hell was she?

Dark. Cold. The cave.

"Do you always snore when you sleep?"

The husky sound of Braddock's voice made her shiver uncontrollably. Or maybe it was the cold. She frowned. "I don't snore." She stood, stretched her legs and then her arms. Sleeping while hugging her knees to her chest had seemed like a good idea in theory. She extended her neck from side to side to work out the kinks.

"Nah, you didn't snore. Just moaned now and then."

Gabrielle stilled. She hoped she hadn't said anything related to the dream she'd had. She wasn't sure Braddock was ready for that much information.

"Must have been dreaming," she said offhandedly

while considering whether or not she wanted to venture out into the woods to relieve herself. It was dark and if she was careful it should be safe enough.

"About me?"

The question had her wheeling back toward the sound of his far too enticing voice. She couldn't see him at all, just comprehended where he was based on hearing his voice. Surely she hadn't really said anything in her sleep. Humiliation stoked in her cheeks when memories from the vivid dream filtered through her mind. Braddock had been making love to her. She shivered again. From the cold, she insisted for the second time.

"Why would I dream about you?" she quipped, infusing the demand with as much *you must be kidding* bluster as she could marshal.

"Maybe because you said my name twice."

A new wave of mortification washed over her. "I have to go out," she said crisply.

"Keep to the right of the cave. Our man on the ridge is still there. He may be using night-vision binoculars now. I imagine desperation is setting in."

Those highly specialized binoculars were incredibly expensive. "What're a bunch of low-life body snatchers doing with technology like that?"

"I wondered the same thing. I think maybe you were right. This isn't just about the slave trade or nabbing a couple of kids for ransom. This is way bigger than that. Some vendetta launched by a powerful enemy."

For once Gabrielle wished she had been wrong. Well, at least the kids were safe.

"Stay crouched close to the ground and don't go far," he advised. "When you get back we'll talk about what our next move should be."

Gabrielle didn't waste any time out in the open. She hugged the rocks as she moved around the cave entry. Kept her head below the level of the thick undergrowth, took care of necessary business as quickly as possible and then got back into that cave.

She settled on the ground near Braddock.

"Another potato? The strawberries and faux carrots are gone, I'm afraid."

Shuddering at the thought but knowing she should eat, she took the couple of knotty little potatoes he offered and forced herself to chew.

"The next few hours will be crucial to their search," Braddock began, speaking quietly, somberly. "The men will be gung-ho and fresh. They'll turn this mountain upside down looking for us. Whoever finds us would be a hero. But as the night goes on they'll grow tired. If they're drinkers, they'll likely booze up. By 2:00 or 3:00 a.m. there won't be a one of them performing at their best. That's when we'll make our move."

She had to give him credit. The plan was ingenuous. He'd thought the whole thing out to the finest detail. Even analyzed the enemy.

"Great plan," she agreed, then countered, "assuming

they don't find us." He hadn't mentioned that scenario. Confidence was a good thing. They were well hidden. There was no reason to think they weren't safe for the time being. And there was always a chance they could go more deeply into the cave. Now there was an idea. Who knew? The cave might be more like a tunnel and offer an exit somewhere on the other side of the mountain. "Should we move deeper into this home away from home? See where it leads?"

"If we're lucky, they won't cover this ground again. And no we can't go any farther. This is it. If this cave ever went any deeper, it fell in ages ago."

So they were either safe or trapped. Depended upon how one wanted to look at it, she supposed. Might as well be an optimist.

"When we make this move, which direction are you proposing we go in? Back toward Sloan's?"

He considered her question a moment before responding. "We can't risk moving back toward the village and since we don't know what lies on the other side of these mountains, and we're not prepared for a long haul, heading back to Sloan's is about our only option. That's what our friends are banking on," he added facetiously.

"So we take the long way back," she offered. "Go way around the expected route."

"Exactly," he concurred, sounding proud that she'd reached the same conclusion. "The journey will take some time and we'll have to go at a frantic pace, but that's our best bet. The only sticking point will be not getting caught at the outset."

"I think we can handle it." She did. Braddock was highly trained. She was prepared on a physical level and damn well willing otherwise. This little bump in the road had forced her to alter her plans a bit, but she wasn't worried. Once she and Braddock were off this mountain, she would give him the slip.

That might not be so easy, the more rational side of her suggested. But there were things she could do in an effort to promote his trust. If he trusted her, he wouldn't be watching her every second of every minute. Trust was key, she decided.

"Let's just hope they don't have any other advanced technology like thermal imaging."

Gabrielle had an idea what that meant and she hoped they didn't, as well. Otherwise there was no way she and Braddock would get out of here alive.

"So we wait some more," she said cheerily.

"That's it."

She might as well put her secondary plan into action. She needed him to believe they were on the same side. Hadn't she rescued Sloan's kids? That fact was likely fresh on his mind. She could build on that.

"I hope Mark and Josh stay out of sight." The statement came out earnestly and she meant it that way. She didn't want those kids hurt. She hated that people used kids for leverage of any kind.

"If the village was the place Sloan had told them to go whenever they were in danger, then the villagers know what they're doing. He's too smart to set up a plan like that otherwise."

His high opinion of Sloan made her anger flare but she kept it to herself. Sloan was no hero. He was a killer. Just like the guys scouring these mountains for them. He'd likely ticked off one or more of them, causing this whole situation in the first place.

"If we can't go anywhere for a while, I guess we might as well do something to pass the time. So, tell me about yourself, Braddock," she prompted, determined to move the conversation away from a man she couldn't discuss openly without letting her real intentions show. "Why aren't you permanently hooked up?" She estimated him to be about thirty-one or two. He was a good-looking guy. Where was the little woman in his life?

"Hooked up?"

She chewed on her lower lip, wishing now she hadn't asked that particular question. She didn't want to hear about how happy he was with whomever. Not that he didn't have a right to be happy but if there was someone else then…

Then what? She couldn't have him? Get real, Gabrielle, she railed. She couldn't have him anyway. Upstanding, career-oriented guys like him didn't go for ex-cons. And that's what she was. Just poor white trash who had, rather ambitiously, lived up to society's expectations. She'd ended up in prison instead of college.

"You know…" she said grouchingly, "who's keeping your bed warm at night? Are you engaged? Divorced? What?"

The dead silence she got in response wasn't at all what she'd been expecting. Had she unknowingly hit a nerve? Had he been married and his wife died? She couldn't stand the suspense.

"Never been married," he revealed. "Never been engaged. My military career was pretty demanding. I didn't have a lot of time for a social life."

Surprised at his answer, she prodded further. "What about now? You've been at the Colby Agency what? Six months?"

She felt like smacking the heel of her hand against her forehead when she heard how she sounded. She had basically just given him the third degree. A dead giveaway. Only someone interested would ask so many questions. What was wrong with her?

Tired. Hungry. Disgusted. Take your pick, she mused.

"I'm new to Chicago. I guess I've been busy settling in."

That was a cop-out if she'd ever heard one. He was evading the question. And now that she'd asked, she might as well have an honest answer.

She tried another tactic. "So you're not dating anyone?"

"What about you?" With those three little words he turned the tables on her.

"Not dating anyone," she said frankly. *I've been too busy plotting Trevor Sloan's assassination,* she didn't add. Her gut twisted with that disgust she'd felt building for days. She told herself it was about the man who was her target, but she'd begun to wonder if it was actually more about her.

"Why not?" Braddock asked. "You're attractive. Smart. Young. Why aren't you out there playing the field?"

She smiled. Moistened her lips and relished his compliments a moment. "You think I'm attractive?"

A really long pause lapsed. "You're not blind, Gabrielle, you must know you are." His words were chosen carefully, uttered with even more caution.

"I can say the same about you," she returned. "Why isn't a handsome guy like you out there on the market?"

He chuckled softly. The sound sent tiny little shivers over her skin. She hated that he could do that so effortlessly.

"Is there a hurry? Is my shelf life about to expire?"

"It's only women who have to worry about expiration dates," she explained impatiently. "Stop beating around the bush, Braddock, answer the question."

"Oh, I see," he said knowingly.

God, she'd give almost anything to be able to see his face. It was driving her absolutely crazy not to be able to use his expression and mannerisms to read what was really on his mind.

"You see what?"

"If you want to go out with me, Gabrielle, just tell me. You don't have to interrogate me."

Embarrassment lit her cheeks. It was a miracle she didn't light up the cave.

"Get real, Braddock. I'm just trying to make conversation here."

"So you're not interested in me, socially or sexually?"

Seething, she propped her elbows on her knees and plunked her chin in her hands. "I give up, Braddock, you're clearly socially inept. A woman can't even carry on a decent dialog with you."

"Gee," he said, amusement in his tone, "it's no wonder I haven't been able to get a date."

GABRIELLE didn't have much to say after that. A.J. figured it was better that way. She'd delved into his personal life a little more deeply than he preferred. He couldn't answer her questions without giving too much information away.

As they sat in the dark saying nothing, time dragging by, he started to feel guilty. She'd tried to be nice and chat. And what had he done? He'd been a hard-ass and had pushed her away. His reasons were valid. His motivation unquestionable. Then why the hell was he feeling guilty for doing what he'd had to do?

"Why did you give up on your appeals when you ended up in prison for someone else's crimes?" That question had been nagging at him since he'd learned the facts about her past. If she were innocent, why hadn't she continued to fight for her freedom?

"Have you ever been poor, Braddock?" she said, her tone sounding bitter.

"No," he said honestly. "We weren't rich by any means, but I never wanted for anything." Certainly not the attention of his parents, of which Gabrielle's childhood had sorely lacked.

"Then you don't know how it feels to be assigned an attorney because you can't afford one, who doesn't care about you and has no choice but to represent you so he's not exactly motivated to go above and beyond the call of duty."

"He didn't believe you were innocent?"

"He only wanted one thing," she said flatly.

Braddock imagined that one thing was to see the case over and done with so he could get back to his real cases, the ones that paid the bigger bucks.

"To sleep with me to make up for not getting paid his usual rate."

Fury drilled through A.J. "He coerced you into having sex with him?" The very idea made him want to kill a man he'd never even met.

"No, he didn't," she said pointedly. "That's why I didn't get an appeal."

A.J. shook his head. Talk about a raw deal. She'd really gotten one. "You couldn't get anyone else to help you?"

"No. People believe what they want to believe. It was easier to pin the drugs and the stolen goods on me. I guess I was just lucky I only did a year and a half of the five."

"Your record while in prison was stellar," he said, knowing how hard it must have been to stay out of trouble inside those walls.

"I guess it's a good thing the parole board didn't know about some of the stuff that actually went on," she said dismissively.

A.J. had heard tales of what went on in prisons, civilian as well as military. Sometimes even good men and women made mistakes, did bad things.

"You don't have to let the past mold your future, Gabrielle." She had tremendous potential as an investigator. What she'd done for those children spoke volumes about her ability to feel compassion for others.

"Easy for you to say, Mr. Ex-Marine. You haven't been where I've been."

"That's true," he admitted. "But you're allowing the past to prevent you from having a future."

"You think he'll kill me."

A.J.'s chest constricted as the words echoed through him. Yes, that was exactly what he thought. But did he tell her that and antagonize her?

"I think he will do whatever necessary to protect his family."

"I don't want to harm his family," she challenged. "Only him."

"You don't think losing their father will harm those two boys you helped rescue from the clutches of those bastards out there hunting us right now?" His own fury stirred. Couldn't she see that her thinking was skewed?

"He took my father away from me." The emotion she felt was tangible.

"Gabrielle, your father took himself away from you long before Sloan killed him. He was never there for you, am I right? He wasn't there for your mother. You didn't even know him."

"Sloan didn't give me the chance," she snarled. "My father had to live the way he did to stay alive."

A.J. sighed. How did he explain to her the way it really was with Gabriel DiCassi? Her mother had fed her a fantasy, apparently, from birth.

"Gabriel DiCassi was an assassin," he stated, not about to pretend on that score. "He wasn't the man you were led to believe he was."

She lunged to her feet. He didn't exactly see it but he felt the movement. He got up himself, just in case her temper got out of control and she attempted to do something stupid like stomp out of the cave.

"You don't know anything about my father. So don't tell me what I should or shouldn't feel."

"You're a smart lady, Gabrielle. Do your research. He was a killer. A cold-blooded killer who got paid well for his evil deeds. That's why he was called *Angel*. That was short for *Angel of Death*."

"That's a lie."

She was closer now. Standing toe-to-toe with him.

"No, it's the truth. Trevor Sloan almost stopped him several years ago when he assassinated a number of business men in Chicago. No one had ever gotten that close to Angel before. Rather than kill Sloan to get him out of his way, Angel did something far worse to get him off his back."

"I don't believe anything you say."

He wanted to touch her. To somehow make her believe his words and, at the same time, to comfort her for what that bastard had done to her.

"He killed Sloan's wife and took his son. At first—" A.J. concentrated hard to recall every detail Victoria had told him "—the authorities thought the child had been murdered, as well. But no body was ever found so no one could be certain. Sloan had to live with that for years. The reality almost drove him crazy. But then he later learned that his son was alive. Angel had given the child to his sister who couldn't have any of her own. That child's name is Mark."

Shock radiated through Gabrielle. Tears burned behind her eyes. "You're lying."

"Why would I? Next time you see Mark, ask him. He has no reason to lie to you."

"Why is Josh with Sloan?" she demanded, a part of

her needing to move beyond Mark and the idea that he'd been taken from his family. "I know he's not Sloan's child." He was her father's child. Gabrielle was certain of that.

"You're right," Braddock said, to her surprise. "Josh is Angel's son. He's your half-brother."

"Why is he with Sloan?" She couldn't be sure if what Braddock told her was the truth but there was always the chance he would be straight up with her. Only she couldn't let him see the impact his words, true or false, had on her.

"Rachel, Sloan's wife, went to the Colby Agency five years ago. She was desperate. Angel wanted to kill her and take the boy. She wasn't afraid to die, but she knew who and what Angel was—he'd murdered her father, used her to get to him. That's how she ended up pregnant with Josh. Rachel would have done anything to protect Josh from Angel. Victoria sent her to Sloan, the one man on the planet who knew anything at all about Angel."

"And he killed him," Gabrielle interjected, her voice tight with emotion.

"That's not exactly true," he said cautiously.

Her instincts stood at attention. "What're you talking about?" It was Sloan who killed her father. She knew that. It had happened at his home.

"There was a woman, Angel's lover-sometimes-partner named Tanya. She's the one who killed your father. Her name was kept out of the press because she turned States' evidence. Her testimony helped to conncct Angcl to numcrous unsolved assassinations."

"How convenient." He had an answer for everything. And now he even had an excuse to get Sloan off the hook. She didn't want to talk about this anymore. Her mother had told her the truth. Why would her mother lie about that? Gabrielle ignored the hesitation that slipped into her determination.

She knew what she knew. This was just a story Victoria Colby-Camp had hatched up to protect Sloan.

"I'm telling you the truth, Gabrielle. Whether you believe it or not, it's all true. Maybe if you give Rachel a chance, she can tell you more. Mark can most likely verify much of what she says."

"I don't want to talk about this anymore." She turned her back on him. Though he couldn't see her face anyway, she wasn't about to risk that he might reach out and feel the tears on her cheeks. Dammit, she hated crying. She was stronger than this.

"All I'm asking you to do, Gabrielle, is to weigh both sides of the story. Consider the sources of each side and decide who and what you can believe for yourself."

His hand settled on her shoulder and she twisted away from his touch. She couldn't deal with that right now. He was just like all the rest. He had an agenda. How had she momentarily forgotten that? He had come here to stop her. To take her back to Chicago where she would likely face charges and end up back in prison. After all, she had three years left on her probation.

It seemed damned convenient that she'd only just now heard about this so-called associate Tanya, her father's real murderer. She folded her arms over her chest and reached for calm. She was supposed to be gaining his trust, not letting him see just how badly she wanted to settle the score with Sloan. She had to get back on track if she expected to regain her freedom.

She sucked it up and did what she had to do. "You're right." She turned back to face him though she couldn't see a damned thing. "I don't have all the facts. I'm stunned that someone else may have been involved with my father's murder and I'm just now hearing about it."

"Getting *all* the facts is important, Gabrielle."

She trembled at the sound of her name on his lips. God, how could she let him get to her like this? As if she had a choice. She'd had no control over this crazy plunge toward obsession with the guy from day one. She'd ordered herself many times to put a halt to the chain reaction. He was too old for her, she'd insisted. Too disciplined. A guy didn't spend more than a decade in the Marines without having some major self-control. But none of those things had slowed her foolish emotional tumble.

It wasn't as if she was in love with him or anything; she just couldn't seem to keep her proper perspective when he was around. No one else had this affect on her.

Why did Victoria have to send him to bring her back?

Anyone else she could have handled ditching without breaking a sweat. But outmaneuvering Braddock would be extremely difficult, especially when her own emotions were working against her.

"When this is over, you have to approach Sloan rationally. It's the right thing to do, Gabrielle." Again he rested his hand on her shoulder. "I'll be right there beside you if that's what you want."

Why would he do that? It was one thing for him to be here. This was his job. No way would he fall down on doing his job. But did he really care how she felt? Or was he playing her the way she intended to play him?

That was the thing with love and all that emotional garbage. People used each other. It was human nature. In her whole life she hadn't been able to trust anyone. Not a single person had ever been there when she needed them most.

That was the truly laughable thing about this situation with Braddock. She knew before she let herself start to obsess about the guy that it was a mistake, and couldn't possibly have a good end. And yet, here she was. Finally in a position to avenge some of the wrongs life had thrown her way and the man she'd stupidly gotten just a little emotionally attached to was the one who stood in her way.

What would happen when he refused to let her

follow through with what she had to do? Could she hurt him? Shoot him, maybe, to clear her path to Sloan?

Frantic shouts outside the cave jerked her attention to the narrow opening.

Braddock's finger came to rest on her lips as he leaned close and whispered in her ear. "Move as far back in the cave as you can. If they come too close I'll make a run for it and divert their attention."

She stared at him through the darkness. Still couldn't see a damned thing. But she didn't have to. It was his words that shook her to the very center of her being.

Who was this guy? He barely knew her, had every reason to believe she was a nutcase considering her prison record and her current agenda. And yet he was willing to risk his life to save hers?

There had to be a catch.

Chapter Nine

A.J. moved nearer to the mouth of the cave and listened to the exchange. At least two men were close by. Too close. One shouted at the other about something A.J. couldn't quite catch well enough to translate. The argument escalated and the men came to blows.

The overindulging had begun. The two fighting outside sounded smashed.

Gabrielle eased up next to him. "What're they doing?" she murmured.

"Arguing over a woman, I think."

Though A.J. couldn't see the two, judging by the sound effects one definitely had the upper hand over the other. The clash wouldn't last much longer.

Gabrielle didn't move away from him immediately as she usually did. Despite having trekked all over these mountains, there was still something intensely feminine about the way she smelled. Sweet and soft, no matter how tough she wanted to pretend to be. She made this dank old cave bearable with her presence.

She wasn't nearly as hard and unfeeling as she wanted the world to believe. All he had to do was to consider the impact she'd had on those boys to know she'd reached out to them in a way the kind of tough woman she pretended to be couldn't hope to do. The boy, Mark, had slipped her a weapon in an attempt to help her out. That spoke volumes about how well they'd connected in the few hours they'd spent together.

He turned to her. "You should stay back, just in case." Just because the two men who'd been fighting had tromped off out of hearing range now didn't mean they or someone else wouldn't be back.

"I'm fine right here."

A smile tugged at his lips. He hadn't noticed how stubborn she was until now. She'd always been so agreeable and ready to do whatever she was told at the agency. He was only now seeing the real Gabrielle. He'd known she was smart and savvy when it came to evaluating cases, but he hadn't expected this fiery side.

Interesting.

He inclined his head and listened, turned his full attention back to the matter at hand: the enemy.

"How much longer before we should make our move?"

Like him, she was growing antsy.

"Soon." He didn't see any reason to put off the inevitable considering his estimations as to the actions of the enemy were already seeing fruition.

The sooner they moved, the sooner they would be out of here and on their way back to safety.

He hoped the talk they'd had would prevent her from doing something they would both regret. He didn't want to see her hurt and his assignment was to ensure that she didn't hurt anyone else. Making a call as to whether she would stick with her promise would be premature. Her actions to this point had been far too volatile for his comfort.

A.J. allowed another half hour to pass before he made the decision to move. It was a no-going-back decision. Once they left the safety of this hidden cave, there might not be another safe haven between here and Sloan's property. But that was a chance they would have to take.

"Ready?"

"Been ready."

He should have expected that answer.

"Don't talk unless absolutely necessary and stay right behind me."

She grabbed him by the shirtsleeve and held him back when he would have moved forward. "Why are you leading? I know the area better than you."

Maybe she did, but most likely she didn't. When he'd been tracking her, he'd paid particular attention to the terrain. He doubted she could say the same. Her goal had been to move quickly toward a specific destination.

"Why don't I lead first and then you can take over later?" Sounded reasonable to him.

"What happened to 'ladies first'?"

Now she wanted to be treated like a lady.

"I thought you preferred being treated like one of the guys," he countered. "Did I get that wrong?"

"Just go, Braddock."

He'd figured that would do the trick.

"Stay close," he reminded.

"Yeah, yeah, I got that part."

A.J. slipped out into the cool night air and held perfectly still for several seconds. He let the night sounds wash over him and carefully filtered all that he heard, the whisper of a breeze, the brush of oak leaves and pine needles and the occasional hoot of an owl. Nothing indicated danger was near.

But a single unintended noise out of him or her, a snapping twig—anything—could bring the enemy out of hiding. They could be hunkered down anywhere. But he was banking on the idea that they wouldn't stop searching for their prey. As long as they were on the move, they could more easily be avoided.

Careful of every step, he moved along the trail rather than pushing through the underbrush. The others would likely be carrying flashlights and could be spotted from a considerable distance. A.J. and Gabrielle were traveling in the dark. But sound carried in the night. They couldn't afford to make even the slightest noise.

A.J. stayed low in an attempt to avoid being spotted by anyone using night-vision binoculars. Gabrielle did the same, instinctively understanding his strategy.

The quarter moon provided just enough illumination to prevent him from leading the way right off a cliff. He paused frequently to listen, then continued his zigzag course eastward and downward.

Heading to his SUV or Gabrielle's Jeep would be a strategic error. Men would be watching the vehicles. That option was out completely. Their only alternative appeared to be to head for Sloan's property via an alternate, unanticipated route. But there was a considerable amount of open ground between the base of the mountains and Sloan's rear gate. The final decision would be best assessed when the time came. Any one of a number of variables could drastically change the necessary strategy.

Gabrielle froze. Strained to hear. She hoped like hell she'd imagined what she'd thought she heard.

Braddock had stopped, as well. He now listened intently, taking his cue from her or having heard the same thing she had.

The sweep of foliage across fabric rasped in the night a second time. Closer this time.

Before she could react Braddock had ushered her down to the ground. He indicated she should stay put while he eased around her position.

Her heart thundered so loudly she couldn't hear

herself think. All it would take was one shout from the guy on their heels…one discharge of a weapon and the others would descend upon them in a flash.

Gabrielle listened intently above the sound of the blood roaring in her ears. Her fingers tightened around the butt of her weapon.

A snap echoed in the night.

No pounding footsteps. No frantic shouts.

The guy hadn't spotted them yet but he was getting closer and closer.

It was all she could do to sit still. She craned her neck to try to see where Braddock was. Did he intend to take the guy down? Was the sound she'd heard from Braddock or the enemy?

Before the hysteria that had started to take root could kick in, Braddock moved up next to her and her eyes closed in relief. Thank God.

"One down. We'll need to keep moving," he whispered, "until we reach the base of the mountain half a mile east of Sloan's property, then we'll double back from the front."

Her toes curled in protest. Sounded like a hell of a lot of walking, and a hell of a lot of risk. But was it the only way to avoid capture? She'd walk just about anywhere to stay alive but the enemy could be hiding anywhere out here in this jungle. Taking out one was good, but there were still nearly a dozen out there.

Since she didn't have a better plan, she went with

Braddock's. She hoped like hell his military background would pay off.

A cold, damp sweat had risen on her skin by the time they reached the lower ridge. She'd slipped so many times and caught herself at the last minute that she wondered how much longer she could possibly avoid that fate. She would hit the ground eventually. It was inevitable.

Braddock stopped. She bumped into his broad back.

He didn't have to say anything. She saw the problem.

Part of the search team had set up camp smack in the middle of the route they wanted to take.

Three men. Campfire. Sleeping bags. Bottle of tequila. Oh yeah, and lots of guns.

Braddock gestured to his right and then started in that direction. Gabrielle, hunkering lower than ever, went after him. They moved along that course for maybe fifteen minutes before encountering more trouble.

Two more men. These two walked aimlessly through the dark. Sentries. One carried a flashlight but appeared more concerned with avoiding obstacles on the ground than with searching for their prey.

Dammit. They were so close to where they needed to be.

Braddock suddenly reached out and cupped the back of her head then pulled her face to his. "We're going to find a place to lay low a little while longer. Okay?"

She trembled before she could stop the reaction, then nodded her agreement.

As he released her, his fingers dragged through her hair and it was all she could do to keep from groaning right there with the enemy breathing down their necks big-time.

Strong-arming her attention back to staying alive, she fell into step behind Braddock.

Wherever he was headed, this time he moved fast. She didn't want to think about what would happen to her if these guys caught up with them. Braddock would likely be shot but her fate wouldn't be so straight-forward, she feared. Shuddering with revulsion, she evicted the possibilities from her mind.

This time Braddock selected a rock outcropping for cover with its sizable nook between the largest of the boulders. He swept his arms around inside first to ensure no critters had gotten the same idea, then settled into the jagged niche. Gabrielle lowered herself into the too-close-for-comfort space next. With both of them ensconced there, he reached out and pulled limbs, leaves, whatever was handy, over the opening.

She tried to settle in and relax, but there was no way she could sit that didn't involve most of her body pressed against his. Complaining would be pointless since the alternative was to risk getting caught.

She mentally admitted defeat and relaxed, allowing her body to contour to his firm frame. Her shoulder was nestled against his chest. Her hip and thigh to his.

This was going to be a very long night.

GABRIELLE CLOSED her eyes and tried to block the dizzying sensations flowing along every nerve ending. A crazy mixture between fear and anticipation.

Every rise and fall of his chest set off a new fizz of sensation. She wasn't sure how she was supposed to get through the next few hours with her mind reeling like this. She shouldn't be feeling this way, shouldn't let her obsession with this man override all else.

She couldn't let him or anything else get in the way of what she had to do.

No matter what he'd told her about her father's murder.

Who knew if there was even a woman named Tanya in her father's history? Sloan could have made the whole thing up to make himself look innocent. Of course his friends would believe him.

She squeezed her eyes more tightly shut, didn't want to think about all that Braddock had told her.

But there was so much she didn't know. Or understand.

Could she trust anything Braddock told her?

Would Mark back up whatever his folks said?

She just didn't want to think about it anymore.

The thought jolted her.

For the first time in more than two years she didn't want to think about getting even. How unbelievable was that?

Not that her plans had changed, she reminded herself. She was just too tired to care right now. She didn't want to think…didn't want to worry….

A.J. FELT GABRIELLE tense against him. He was pretty damned tense himself. The feel of her warm body pressed firmly along his was playing havoc with his ability to think straight.

Trying to block his reaction to her nearness would be futile. Instead he lay there, tried to relax and let his male responses do what they would. Even the dull ache that had started deep in his skull couldn't detract from the buzz in the rest of his being.

He thought about the conversation they'd had regarding who killed her father. She had been startled to learn someone else might be involved. She hadn't believed him, but the news had given her pause.

Her alcoholic mother had sure as hell done a number on Gabrielle. A major disservice. He wasn't sure if anything he could say would convince her to trust him much less to believe what he told her. But he had to keep trying. If she went after Sloan, she wouldn't survive.

A.J. couldn't let that happen. Keeping her from reaching Sloan was his job, but letting this tragedy go down would be a travesty in and of itself. He couldn't let it happen. And he wouldn't let her ruin the rest of her life because of the fantasies her mother had spun.

Her mother had lied; maybe even convinced herself that the stories she'd told were the truth.

Technically it wasn't his job to undo the damage Gabrielle had suffered, but he wanted to. He wanted her to have the kind of future she deserved. She was too smart to be stuck back in prison.

He had known men like her in the Marines. Guys who hadn't had the first advantage growing up. A.J. knew the story too well. No parental guidance. Difficulty making good friends. The friends she had managed to make were less than desirable. But she'd worked with what she had. Despite the lack of parental support, she'd managed to make good grades and get accepted to college. And then the final straw in the burden she carried had been dropped like a bomb. The fantasy father she'd dreamed of was dead. No chance of ever meeting him, much less knowing him. And worse, the media painted a picture of an evil killer, the exact opposite from what she'd been told.

So Gabrielle chose denial. Her mother would not have lied to her. Though that same mother could have cared less if she'd lived or died most days.

The little girl's one dream was shattered. A crappy life held together by one fleeting fantasy was shot to hell.

So the little girl decided to get even with the world by having her revenge on the man who'd ended her fantasy.

A.J. turned his face slightly in a futile attempt to make out her profile. She was reaching for the only thing that felt right, felt noble in her life. And no matter that she looked like a very grown-up woman, gorgeous figure included, a whole lot of that little girl still lived deep down inside her. A little girl who just needed somebody to love her.

"You know, Braddock," she said quietly, her words startling him all the same, "I haven't had sex in like six months. If you keep this up we may have a serious problem on our hands."

Damn. Was he that obvious? Even in the dark?

"I was just thinking," he admitted, keeping his voice down to a whisper. The *plat-plat-plat* overhead informed him that it had started to rain. That could be good, he decided. It could send their enemy into fixed camps. The large groups in camps they could spot and go around.

"I have a pretty good idea what you were thinking," she retorted knowingly.

He ordered his body to relax. They were pressed so close together she could feel his tension rising in a very palpable form.

"Sometimes we have no control over primitive instinct," he suggested. "You can rest assured it wasn't an intellectual decision."

"It rarely is."

That she so fully understood his reaction irritated

him beyond reason. "Let's just try to get through this, shall we."

She shrugged. "Sure. Just let me know if you decide you need to take matters in hand. I'm not into voyeurism."

Now that ticked him off.

He shifted onto his side so that he could look more directly at her lying next to him. Not that it did any good since he couldn't see a damned thing.

"Don't give yourself so much credit, Gabrielle. The situation isn't that hard."

She made a breathy sound that was basically a laugh. "From where I sit, it feels pretty damned hard."

The irritation morphed into fury, but before he could say what was on his mind a noise, ten maybe fifteen yards away, nabbed his attention.

He felt Gabrielle stiffen.

Rustling foliage. The crinkle of leaves under a booted foot. They didn't actually have to worry about being seen, getting stepped on would be the more probable scenario.

A.J. held his breath. Listened.

The two, maybe three men stopped almost on top of them.

Their dialogue sounded weary with disgust. A.J. could make out most of what was said. The men—definitely two, he decided—were furious over having to tromp around the woods in the rain. In their opinion the man and woman were long gone. A.J. hoped this was the prevailing attitude among their pals.

This could be good news for A.J. and Gabrielle. The less interest the men had in their work, the poorer the job performance.

The conversation shifted to business.

According to the man who sounded as if he might have seniority over his *compadre,* all they needed to make the deal happen was the children. The interlopers—he and Gabrielle, A.J. surmised—were of no real consequence. The other guy argued that they might not be able to find the children in time unless they found A.J. and Gabrielle. The truth could be gotten out of them and finding the children would be a simple matter.

Someone they referred to as *jefe* wouldn't wait beyond the forty-eight hours he had given.

A.J. knew *jefe* translated to boss. These two felt certain they would all be killed if the children weren't brought in within that forty-eight hour deadline. From the discussion, it appeared the emphasis of the search was on the older child, the younger somehow more insignificant. A.J. wondered at this. Was it because Mark, the oldest, was Sloan's flesh and blood?

The two moved away, the conversation fading with their footsteps.

"Why do you think they want Mark?" Gabrielle whispered.

She'd apparently understood most of the conversation, as well.

"I don't know. But we're going to have to make sure they don't find them."

"How can we find out who this *jefe* is?"

A.J. wasn't about to tell her, but he knew of only one way. Infiltrate the enemy. In his experience, in a situation like this one, there was only one way to do that.

Get caught.

Gabrielle could sense a change in Braddock's demeanor. The tension in his body felt different somehow. Resolved or resigned. The sexual tension was still there but far less noticeable. Had he understood more of the conversation than she had? There had been blocks of dialogue that had gone right over her head, but she'd felt confident she'd gotten the most important parts.

If he was plotting something and leaving her out... how would she know until it was too late? She had to find a way to keep him off balance where she was concerned.

There was only one way she could think of to do that.

She purposely eased her hip against him. His body reacted instantly. No point in him denying that he was attracted to her, she could feel that he was.

"We'll stay here a little longer, then we'll try to cover some more ground," he murmured, his voice sounding oddly strained.

"Are you sure it's a good idea for us to attempt to

move about in the darkness? Shouldn't we just stay right here?" As she said this she put a little more pressure on that sensitive location.

"No." His voice croaked. "We have to move."

She had to smile. Men. Their physical reactions were as dependable as time itself.

"I'm cold," she said next. "Is it okay if we lay a little closer?" She'd no sooner asked the question than she pushed her arms around him and snuggled closer.

"Er…sure." He hesitated but eventually wrapped his arms around her.

She had to admit, she liked the feel of him. Muscular, powerful. He was very fit. A woman wouldn't have to worry about not being safe with him. She imagined he could hold his own in most any situation.

The minutes ticked by like hours. The rain plopped on the leaves of the trees and the underbrush. Even the fresh smell of rain couldn't detract from the smell of *him*.

Gabrielle had quickly come to regret her move. His body wasn't the only one responding to various stimuli. Like the feel of his every male contour nestled against her more pliable frame. His chest felt like a rock wall with her breasts flattened there save for the nipples that had gone rock-hard themselves.

The equally solid ridge below his belt had her lower anatomy humming with anticipation. She had denied herself for so damned long that even the idea of having sex with Braddock made her melt in readiness.

Maybe she should just stop neglecting herself and have sex with him right now.

Need jolted through her.

They could die most any minute, she might as well have a little fun first.

It didn't seem right somehow to lay here hiding from killers and not take advantage of the one luxury offered by the situation.

Sex with Braddock would be good. He was older than her, which translated into more experience. Older guys knew what women wanted more so than younger guys who were far too concerned with themselves to care what a woman needed.

"Braddock," she whispered, "I think—"

"Don't talk," he ordered. The feel of his lips against her temple sent a thrill through her.

She tilted her head back and attempted to align her lips with his. "Talking wasn't what I had in mind."

His breath whispered against her lips. His mouth couldn't be more than two or three centimeters from hers and yet he held back…denied her contact.

"Not a good idea," he said tightly.

She lifted slightly, closed that meager distance, allowing her lips to brush his.

"Oh, yeah," she challenged, "this is a very good idea."

His mouth came down hard over hers as he pinned her to the ground with his weight. At almost the same instant his hips ground into hers and it was all she could do not to cry out with the exquisite pleasure of the resulting sensations.

Leaves and dirt trickled down onto her face but she didn't care. She just wanted to feel this…to feel him. His kiss was relentless and filled with a kind of desperation that matched her own.

She opened her mouth in invitation when what she wanted was to spread her legs and be taken completely with the same desperation with which he kissed her.

His tongue plunged into her mouth and she whimpered.

He froze.

She could feel his heart pounding…could hear his breath raging in and out of his lungs…but above all else she felt his emotional withdrawal.

"We can't do this now." His voice was taut, as ragged as his respiration.

"I guess this is something else we'll just have to finish later," she said breathlessly, determined to keep him guessing.

He plunged the fingers of his right hand into her hair and cradled her head. "I can guarantee," he said, his tone a blatant warning, "that we will finish this part."

He made no move to roll off her. Instead he stayed right there, his weight pressing down on hers.

She paid dearly for her little ploy.

Over and over again.

Chapter Ten

It was almost dawn. In her office, Victoria stood at the window that overlooked the city she loved. She hadn't been able to sleep. Some part of her, that instinctive part that had kept her awake so many nights after she lost her son, warned that whatever was happening in Mexico was getting worse instead of better.

A.J. had left more than forty-eight hours ago and still there was no word from him. Amy Calhoun had followed twenty-four hours later. Sloan and Rachel were still away and no one appeared to have any idea where.

This was very wrong.

Something well beyond Gabrielle Jordan's need for revenge.

The telephone on her desk rang. Victoria turned to verify that it was her private line. It would be Lucas. No one else used that number. Well, except for Jim or Tasha, and it was far too early for a call from either of them.

Unless there was a problem with the baby.

A new kind of fear rushed through Victoria's heart as she hurried to grab the receiver.

Tasha was only a few months along but each trimester in a pregnancy carried its own set of risks and difficulties.

"Victoria Colby-Camp," she said, her voice breathless.

"I do love to hear you say that."

Lucas.

Relief whirred along her nerve endings. "Lucas, you're calling awfully early." That meant that he knew she wasn't at home in bed as she should be. He worried that she worked too hard. As if he had any room to talk.

"And you're at the office rather early," he countered gently.

The fact that she missed him immensely could very well be part of the reason she couldn't sleep. Whenever he went back to D.C. to advise on a situation, she felt completely out of sorts.

"I miss you," she admitted, partly because it was true and partly because she wanted to shift the focus from her to him. "Will you be back this week as planned?"

He sighed. Not a good sign.

"It's looking like next week. Do I need to cut it short? Tell them they'll have to do this without me?"

Victoria smiled. He would do that, too. Lucas would lay down his life for her, here and now if she asked him to. He would gladly come home early and never regret the decision or question her reasons if she asked him to. He was truly one of a kind.

"No. No. I'll be fine."

"Still no word from Sloan, I take it," he guessed.

"Nothing. I'm concerned, Lucas. This feels very wrong somehow. Very, very wrong."

"Braddock is a good man, Victoria. He can handle Gabrielle."

He was right. She had no doubt about A.J.'s ability to get the job done. It was that nagging feeling that this was bigger than Gabrielle...far bigger than they knew...that bothered her.

"Do me a favor, my dear," Lucas urged.

Another smile tilted her lips. "Yes." She knew what he would say even before he uttered the words. *Please take care of yourself...you know I couldn't live without you.*

"This case is personal to you. I know you're worried. But, please take care of yourself...you know I couldn't live without you."

She promised her husband she would take the best of care of herself, told him she loved him and said goodbye. Her life had gone so well for months now. Her son and his wife were happy. Her first grandchild was on the way. Lucas was amazing. Life just couldn't get any better. Perhaps having it all after years of personal loss and suffering made the prospect of disaster even more painful.

Borrowing trouble wouldn't help. She had to trust her incredible staff to do what they did best.

Determined to get on with her day, despite the early hour, she strode across her office with the lounge as her destination. A strong cup of coffee would help lift her spirits. She'd had a cup before leaving the house. But that caffeine fix had long ago worn off. Time for another.

Three or four minutes was all it took for the coffee-maker to do its business. The smell of fresh-brewed coffee filled the air and she felt better already. After pouring a steaming cup, she cradled it in her hands a moment to relish the warmth then sipped the smooth blend Mildred Parker, her personal assistant, special-ordered every week like clockwork.

As she strolled along the hall, headed back to her office, she was surprised to see Ian Michaels striding purposely in that same direction.

"Good morning, Victoria."

Daylight had scarcely started to creep across the dark sky. That she was here so early wasn't so shocking considering her husband was out of town and her relationship to Sloan wouldn't let her treat this like just another case. But Ian Michaels' appearance at this hour meant something was up. Something tangible. Not just intuition.

"We have a problem," she suggested as they entered her office together.

"I believe so."

Anticipation sent her heart into a faster rhythm. "Why don't you have a seat and bring me up to speed."

Ian settled into one of the wing chairs that flanked her desk and wasted no time in getting to the point. "I've spent most of the night attempting to reach Amy. Despite a call on the hour, every hour, there is no answer at Sloan's residence."

Worry sliced deep into Victoria's chest. "When was the last time you made contact?"

"Shortly after her arrival yesterday. Around noon. The house was deserted and she'd had no luck touching base with A.J."

"She hasn't attempted to call in and you haven't been able to reach her?" Victoria reiterated, worry gnawing at her with even more ferocity now.

"Correct."

"All right then." Victoria set her coffee aside and folded her hands on her desk. "We'll need to go in this time under the assumption the area is hostile."

"I agree." Ian leveled his gaze on hers. "Ric Martinez and I will leave this morning. Since he's fluent in the language, I felt he would be an asset."

Victoria nodded. "Excellent decision." She considered Ian a moment. "You haven't been in the field in a while, Ian, are you sure this is what you want to do? There are other well qualified investigators to choose from."

The determination that glimmered in his eyes told

Victoria that further discussion was not only unnecessary but a waste of time.

"I trained Amy personally. If her disappearance is related to a failure on my part—"

"Ian," Victoria cut in, "that won't be the case. However, I understand your need to do this personally. You do whatever you need to. We always take care of our own."

Ian stood. "We'll contact you as soon as we've arrived at our destination."

Victoria watched him go. For most of her life she had been able to rely on her intuition.

Considering what she feared, this was one time when she would just as soon that instinct failed her.

Chapter Eleven

A.J. stopped. Listened. The rain was still falling. Slipping down the leaves of the trees and dripping onto their heads. He ignored it.

He hadn't heard anything out of the men searching for them since before daylight. Since he and Gabrielle had climbed out of that hole. He'd spent the whole night on the verge of ripping her clothes off and...

Don't think about it, he reminded himself.

She'd pushed the issue, in the hope of keeping him off balance, he felt certain. She'd had him armed and ready from the moment she scooted in next to him. He deserved a medal for maintaining control all those hours.

They'd been moving for just over an hour. It was daylight now. Still no cell phone service. Using it would be a risk considering the enemy appeared to be equipped with the unexpected as far as technology went. Touching base with Amy wasn't necessary at this point. A.J. had a plan. The first step of which was to get the hell off this mountain without getting caught.

"Did you hear that?"

Her desperate whisper had him turning to face Gabrielle. He had avoided doing that for the past hour.

A sound echoed in the distance. He cocked his head and listened. A frown furrowed his brow as he strained to hear, but couldn't identify the noise.

"Damn," she moaned.

Their gazes locked as recognition simultaneously slammed into their brains.

"Dogs."

She grabbed his hand. "We have to run!"

A.J. plunged forward, pulling her along behind him. There was no time to discuss the issue or to consider other options. The baying howls grew louder with each passing second. There were no other options.

They pushed through the thick growth and the gray mist still hanging in the early morning air. The dampness surged in and out of his lungs as he pushed harder, careful of the sudden twists and turns in the path that wound around chillingly steep cliffs. One wrong step and the race would be over.

Loose rock combined with the wet earth made going hazardous at best. A.J. kept her hand tightly clasped in his own. He couldn't afford to slow down and yet their efforts would be for naught if he didn't find a way to get those dogs off their scent.

Another sound distracted him momentarily. Just ahead. Water. A few more yards and A.J. skidded to a halt. Beyond the precipice where they stood, a waterfall rushed over the cliffs of the opposite rock face. The water fell for a hundred feet or more, some of it atomizing into mist before it hit a large plunge pool on the canyon floor below. The wildflowers and conifers all around gave the place a serene-like ambience. But the dogs howling in the distance shattered that lovely vision.

The plan materialized instantly. He knew what he had to do. Protecting the children, as well as Gabrielle, was his primary objective.

"Give me your sweatshirt."

She started at the demand. Looked up at him as if she'd just snapped out of a trance the incredible view had lured her into.

"My sweatshirt? Why do—"

"This is the bottom line, Gabrielle. No way can we get out of here together. Not with those dogs on our trail," he said before she could interrupt. "One of us has to get word of what's really going on to the agency."

She looked increasingly skeptical.

"Whatever your original agenda," he said, understanding what was going through her mind, "right now the main goal has to be protecting the children." He knew she wouldn't argue with that.

"What does my sweatshirt have to do with your plan?" She looked outright suspicious now.

"One of us has to play decoy while the other gets away."

"I'll be the decoy," she challenged. "I can run faster than you anyway."

For two seconds A.J. wondered how the woman who wanted to have her vengeance on a man like Sloan could offer up her life to save someone else's. Didn't add up. He wondered if she understood that yet.

"Give me the sweatshirt, Gabrielle," he ordered. "We don't have time to argue or we'll both end up dead."

She glanced past him, in the direction of the yowling that grew ever closer, chewed her lip as if she couldn't decide what was the right thing to do.

"Men," she huffed. "They think they're the only ones who can play the hero."

She ripped off her sweatshirt, leaving a form-fitting tee behind. Before he could stop himself his gaze had dropped to her breasts.

She flung the shirt at him. "What am I supposed to do?"

"I'll keep going," he explained, dragging his attention back to her face. "I'll drag your shirt behind me so that the dogs don't miss your scent."

"Yeah, yeah, I get that part."

"You…" He hoped she wouldn't have a problem with this part. They were running out of time. He couldn't risk her getting caught. If she couldn't withstand the interrogation, she might just give up the location of the children. "You jump into the water below and stay out of sight until they've passed. Be sure to wait ample time. You don't want one of the dogs picking up your scent and turning back."

She waved her hands back and forth as if to erase all that he'd just said. "Wait just a minute." She hitched her thumb toward the cliff behind her. "You want me to jump in there." She glanced down. "I don't think so."

"It's not that far from this side. The water is deep."

Her gaze swung back to him, her eyebrows raised in obvious skepticism. "And you would know this how?"

"By the way the water in the pool reacts when the water from the falls hits it." He looked back as the sound of the pursuing dogs grew even louder. "Trust me, Gabrielle, I wouldn't have you jump if it wasn't safe. It's not nearly as far down on this side." He reached behind him and withdrew her 9 mm from his waistband at the small of his back. "You might need this." He shoved the weapon into her waistband, next to her bellybutton. He trembled inside as the back of his hand grazed her flat belly.

Gabrielle couldn't believe she was doing this. For one thing, he had just outlined a suicide mission for himself, maybe even for her. But it was the only way to see that one of them survived without capture. She understood that.

"All right. But don't hold it against me when they catch your ass."

He grinned, a totally lopsided gesture that took her

breath away. "The only thing I'll hold against you is the way you tortured me this morning in that damned hole."

"Like you said, Braddock," she quipped, time was short, she had to do this, "that's just another thing we'll have to finish when this is done."

She wanted to grab him and kiss the hell out of him. Just looking into those eyes made her ache with yearning. But there was no time. She pivoted on her heel and, without bothering to assess the situation further, jumped.

The cool mist-filled air rushed upward around her as she plummeted toward the foaming pool. The water's cold embrace enveloped her as she sliced into it.

Down, down, down she plunged. She arched her body and kicked hard. Harder and harder she kicked, forcing herself upward, away from the rocky bottom of the natural pool.

But she didn't surface immediately.

Cutting through the cold water, she swam toward the rock wall. Her lungs burned with the need to drag in a breath of air.

Not yet, she ordered. Just hold on.

She couldn't remember the last time she'd swam, much less dived. But when lives were on the line, a person could do most anything.

Stroking harder still, she finally reached the rock wall that surged up to where she'd left A.J. standing.

She surfaced. Coughed. Gasped for air.

She blinked, looked around to get her bearings. An inset in the mountain allowed the pool to slip beneath the rocks, like an underground cave with about two feet of space between the surface of the water and the rock ceiling overhead.

When she'd caught her breath, she dared to edge closer to the opening. She treaded water just enough to keep her head above the surface and listened.

The dogs were close. Not directly overhead but very close.

As her heart slowed to a normal rhythm, she silently prayed that Braddock would outmaneuver his pursuers.

She almost laughed when she considered that she'd just prayed. She couldn't remember the last time she'd prayed. Maybe it was after that time she'd gone to Sunday school with a friend from school—one of the few normal friends she'd had. She'd listened to the priest talk about how important it was to pray for for-giveness among other things. She'd come home psyched about talking to God. Her mother had scoffed in her face and proceeded to explain how prayer wasn't for people like them. God didn't bother listening to those who couldn't tithe or didn't attend church.

Gabrielle had cried that night. She'd been twelve. As far as she could remember it was the last time she'd ever cried. She'd decided her mother was right. And after that she stopped caring a little…maybe a lot.

What was she doing going there? She banished the

memories and focused on the here and now. Shouting echoed into the canyon along with the howling of the dogs. Damn. They were practically on top of her now.

Should she duck back under the water?

Not taking any chances, she eased deeper beneath the craggy overhang. No way was she going to risk getting caught and render Braddock's sacrifice moot. She owed him her best effort. She had to get out of here and call for help.

Then she could finish her business with Sloan.

She couldn't make out any of the shouted words above the barking. But she could hear them tearing through the foliage, the dogs as well as the men. She struggled to make out how many men...three...four.

Maybe more.

As hard as she tried to block the images, her mind created the pictures and she just couldn't stop them. He knew he wouldn't be able to get away. It wasn't as though he could climb a tree and escape. Who knew if there would be another pool to disappear into up ahead? Not likely. She'd been over this terrain and this was the only waterfall she'd encountered.

Braddock was screwed.

Those guys would interrogate him and when they didn't get what they wanted...he would die.

Her stomach clenched at the idea.

Tired of treading water, she held on to a jutting rock. She had to get back to Sloan's and give Amy a heads-up on what was going on and then she was going to track down these sons of bitches and kick their asses.

Surely, Braddock could hold out for a few hours. She doubted they would kill him until they had the location of the children. He would recognize that. Hell, he was an ex-marine. He'd probably kill at least two of them before they gave up on him anyway.

Following Braddock's final orders, she waited until the sound of the dogs diminished in the distance. Then she glided through the water to the closest shore. She scrambled onto the lush bank and got to her feet.

Taking a moment to get her bearings, she drew in a couple of deep breaths. Go back the way they came or head in the direction of the hunters?

Well, she'd never been a Girl Scout so looking for which way the moss grew on the rocks wouldn't help. And it wasn't dark, so she couldn't look for the North star. But her instincts told her to go back the way she'd come until she found something she'd encountered before and recognized. Always worked in her favorite video game.

A.J. DIDN'T BREAK his stride in spite of the treacherous terrain. A scream behind him let him know that one of the men chasing him hadn't made the twisting descent as easily as A.J. Also lucky for him, they were all pathetic shots.

Or maybe he'd just been lucky so far.

The men likely had orders not to shoot to kill. They

needed the children's location and killing him wouldn't give them that.

Getting caught wasn't something he could avoid. He wasn't cocky enough to think he would get out of this. What he needed was to lure them as far away from Gabrielle as possible.

He was counting on her to get back to civilization, whether it was Sloan's residence or back to Florescitaf, to get a call through to the Colby Agency. Victoria needed to understand what was really going on down here.

A branch slapped him in the face and his eyes burned, but he didn't let it slow him down.

The incline dipped downward sharply, the goat trail he followed twisting dangerously. A.J. pushed harder, didn't let his mind dwell on the risk. Dead was dead. He could go this way or he could endure hours, maybe days, of torture.

His right foot slipped on a scattering of loose rock, the surface beneath damp from the rain that had finally stopped. He scrambled for purchase. Couldn't quite make it. He went down on his butt. Bounced down the slope, almost bounded over the edge of the cliff.

Digging into the rocky earth with his fingers, he dragged himself back onto the ledge.

The snarling and barking of the dogs was louder.

He had to get moving.

His heart thumping against his sternum, he raced

downward. He didn't have to look at his hands to know they were skinned and bleeding.

The ping of a bullet bounced off a rock next to his knee. Close. Too damned close.

He glanced over the edge of the ledge…considered what might lay beyond the trees and underbrush visible.

Might as well find out.

He jumped.

He hit the ground rolling. Saplings, bushes, rocks, he spun over and over and through a tangle of nature's barriers. A tree stopped his tumble. Knocked the breath out of him.

Doubling over, he coughed and sucked in a breath. Couldn't just lay here. He clamored to his feet and started to run again. Through the bushes. Plummeting more than running. His control over his descent was nonexistent.

But he couldn't give up, had to keep going.

It wasn't until he fell again that he realized how weak his legs had grown.

When he stopped tumbling downward, rolled to a jarring stop, he looked down at himself. Blood oozed from his right side.

Damn.

He'd been hit, after all.

The sound of the dogs howling and shouted voices tugged his gaze upward.

He had company.

He tried to get up…couldn't do it.

Well, hell.

He closed his eyes and surrendered to the inevitable.

Trampling foliage and curt Spanish echoed around him. He ignored the demands. Didn't get up as he was ordered. Let them think he was unconscious.

A kick in the ribs made him grunt but he still didn't respond to their demands.

The metal-on-metal slide of a 9 mm being readied for firing didn't do the trick, either.

If they shot him now it would save them both a lot of trouble.

But life was never that simple.

GABRIELLE PLUNGED through the woods. She'd found the original trail she'd taken when leading the boys from their initial hiding place to the village. All she had to do was to keep going and she would reach the area near where she'd left the Jeep in ten maybe fifteen minutes.

She gasped for breath, felt as if her lungs would explode for sure. But she couldn't slow down. Her clothes were still wringing wet and her body felt numb with exhaustion.

She couldn't think about Braddock right now. She'd heard the gunshots.

Worry twisted inside her.

Surely they wouldn't kill him…not yet.

Call Victoria first. She would know what to do. Then

try to pick up the trail of the guys who had taken Braddock. He wouldn't like that part of her plan, but too bad. She wasn't about to leave him to the wolves.

Her feet slipped out from under her and she bounced down a steep ridge on her bottom. When her bumpy journey ended, she struggled to her feet, grimacing with pain. Damn she would have scrapes and bruises big-time.

As she neared the place where she'd parked the Jeep, she slowed down and caught her breath. If someone was still watching her Jeep, she didn't want to be caught.

She wiped her face with her arm and scanned the area. She didn't see anyone, but that didn't mean there wasn't someone there, hiding, waiting for her to show up.

Slowly, noiselessly, she inched her way toward the Jeep.

She froze when she saw the lone guard leaned against the rear bumper of her Jeep.

Swearing softly, she considered her options.

She couldn't shoot him, it would make too much noise.

She couldn't take him physically, he was much bigger than her. Stronger, too.

But if she could sneak up behind him, she could whack him over the head and at least render him unconscious.

She could do that. No problem.

As she eased closer to her target, she looked around for the right kind of weapon. A nice, heavy rock, but not so heavy that she couldn't wield it with enough force.

The crackle of a voice over a walkie-talkie shattered the silence.

Gabrielle stilled, listened.

The orders to the man were given in Spanish and Gabrielle didn't get much of these. She caught "hurry" and "return" but nothing else.

The guard agreed to whatever he'd been told. When the call ended, to her supreme astonishment he gathered his stuff, a bag and a rifle, and started off into the mountains.

To rendezvous with his *compadres?*

She couldn't say for sure. But rather than risk it, she sat still and watched him go.

When he'd disappeared over the ridge she finally moved, using extreme caution. When she'd reached her Jeep, she looked inside and found her stuff still there. Incredible. Money, passport, everything was right where she'd left it. Everything but the keys to the Jeep.

She slung the shoulder strap of her bag over her head and quietly closed the door to the Jeep. If she really tried, she might be able to hot-wire it. She'd watched it done a couple of times. But taking the vehicle would be a dead giveaway that she'd escaped. It would be best for the bad guys to believe she was dead. That she'd fallen over the cliffs or something like that. Or that she was lost.

Why would they bother looking for her body if they had a live one they could question?

She could walk back to Sloan's and take one of the cars from there. Pablo's or something from the garage. All she had to do was to get there.

When she reached the last of the trees and any decent cover, she hunkered down and surveyed the terrain. It wasn't noon yet…nine or ten o'clock maybe.

She looked down at her clothes. The khakis and filthy T-shirt would blend with the sand, but not her dark hair.

What the hell?

She peeled off the T-shirt, leaving her nude-colored bra. Careful to get all of her hair hidden, she twisted the tee into a turban. Good enough.

The shoulder bag wasn't a problem since it was the natural-colored crocheted type anyway.

She took a long look around the terrain between her and Sloan's property once more and then did what she had to do.

She ran like hell, careful to keep her head low.

She didn't slow down until she'd reached the rear gate. Despite the early hour, the sun felt hot on her back. The sand warm beneath her feet.

After she'd reached the gate, she tugged the T-shirt back on and retrieved her handgun, the one Braddock had given back to her. She still had the .38 that Mark had given her tucked into her sock. She hoped she wouldn't need a backup piece but she might.

She moved through the gate, careful to stay against the wall. No sudden moves. No noise.

Voices echoed from somewhere beyond the building on the back of the property.

Spanish.

Damn.

She should have thought of this. If they were watching the vehicles, they would be watching this house.

Great.

Now what did she do?

She needed to get inside to a phone.

Wait.

Amy Calhoun was supposed to be here.

A new kind of uncertainty washed over Gabrielle.

Had she walked into this trap? Or was she watching from a distance?

This thing just kept getting more and more complicated.

Didn't anyone understand she had an agenda of her own?

Amy was young. Not much older than Gabrielle. She'd just gotten married. What, last year?

The girl was seriously in love. So was her husband. Gabrielle had met him once.

If something happened to Amy…

Okay. She had to determine if Amy was even here. She couldn't do anything else until she verified that aspect of the situation.

Holding her breath, Gabrielle eased around the corner of the building. As she did, she considered that she'd already risked her life for two kids...now here she was taking a chance on getting shot for a woman she barely knew.

She hadn't come here to rescue people.

Whatever.

Now wasn't the time to worry about what she couldn't change.

Moving across the courtyard would be a major mistake. She surveyed the way the house folded in around the pool and a portion of the courtyard. If she got inside, she could move from room to room with at least some cover.

An open window at the far right of the house suggested opportunity. All she had to do was to reach it.

She hadn't seen any of the men whose voices she could hear just yet. Maybe they were all inside.

She slipped toward the west wing of the house. When no bullets started to fly and no unexpected shouts were screamed her way, she figured the men were distracted by something else.

Lucky for her.

She peeked into the room first. Bedroom. Toys. Josh's maybe. She climbed inside and took a few seconds to ascertain her position relative to that of the enemy.

Sounded as if they were in the east wing...several rooms away.

This was one big house.

Gabrielle stood at the door for a full minute before

she worked up the nerve to move out into the hall. She'd never considered herself a coward, but this was hard.

During those gut-wrenching moments she found herself admiring Josh's room. He had everything a little boy could want. He'd been so much luckier than her…but she was glad.

Moving slowly, carefully, she eased past room after room. Thankfully all were empty.

As she neared the main living area, the voices grew louder.

She sniffed the air and decided they were eating.

Her pulse racing, Gabrielle crouched as low as possible and moved into the entry hall. This was as close as she dared get. The men alternated between speaking in Spanish and in butchered English. The gist of the conversation revolved around the fact that the man—*Braddock* she understood—had been captured. The woman—*her*—hadn't been found.

The search had been called off. They didn't care if the woman died on that mountain. They had what they needed now.

She couldn't help smiling as she considered that they didn't have anything because Braddock would die before he would talk.

Her smile faded.

She didn't want him to die.

It went way beyond mere human compassion.

She had feelings for him.

Foolish feelings. Pointless feelings.

But they were there just the same.

Just another screwup in a long line of mistakes in her poor excuse for a life.

She inclined her head and listened to the man, who sounded as if he were in charge, lay out his next orders.

He'd gotten news that a private plane had landed in an airfield near Chihuahua. He suspected it might be more of Sloan's friends. His men were to load up and leave now before the interlopers arrived.

Uncertainty charged through Gabrielle.

What did she do?

If they left, she wouldn't know where to look for Braddock. She was supposed to make that call. But what if they got away...

She made a decision.

She had to go with them.

They just couldn't know they had a stowaway.

While the men prepared to leave, she slipped out the front door.

She held her breath until she verified that no one was watching the vehicles.

There were two trucks, an SUV and a cargo-type van.

The van looked like the best bet.

She surveyed the parking area and dashed across the cobblestone. She didn't breathe again until she'd flattened against the back of the van.

The sound of a door opening somewhere beyond

her position had her climbing into the van without another second's hesitation.

She eased the door closed, flinching as the metal lock clicked into place.

Turning around in the dark, she wished like hell she had Mark's pocket-size flashlight.

Feeling her way, she moved toward the front of the vehicle. The cargo area was closed off from the passenger area. Good thing. She hadn't even thought of that.

Her fingers encountered fabric. She felt the material and decided it was a tarp of some sort.

The front doors of the van opened. The vehicle shifted as passengers settled into the seats up front.

Gabrielle didn't move a muscle until the doors had closed, the engine had started and the van moved. She could barely make out the muffled voices of the driver and his passenger. The one driving said something about going back to the compound, then the volume of the radio was cranked up.

Wherever that was, Gabrielle hoped it was the same place they would take Braddock.

Something moved beyond the tarp.

Gabrielle held still…didn't even breathe.

A faint whimper pierced her fear.

She scrambled over to the far corner of the van and gasped as her hands found someone huddled in the corner. Female. Long hair. Gabrielle felt for the woman's hands. They were restrained. Then she touched her face. Her mouth was taped shut. The woman whimpered again.

Her heart thundering, Gabrielle whispered, "Don't scream. I'm going to take the tape off your mouth."

The woman nodded.

The instant Gabrielle removed the tape, the woman said in a whispered rush, "Gabrielle, you have to help me!"

It was Amy Calhoun from the Colby Agency.

With her captured and Gabrielle stuck in here with her, who would call for help?

Chapter Twelve

As the temperature rose outside so did the heat index inside the van. Sweat dampened Gabrielle's skin. The stench of waste and pure filth, whether human or animal she couldn't say, permeated the interior, the intensity rising with the temperature.

The ride lasted for what felt like hours, but may only have been minutes. Gabrielle could no longer judge something as trivial as the passage of time. She recognized the problem. Fatigue and a mild case of shock. The events weren't supposed to affect her to such an extent, but they had all the same.

She'd thought that her dysfunctional childhood and time in prison had prepared her for most anything but she'd been wrong. So damned wrong.

The image of the man she'd been forced to kill intruded into her musings. The blood pooled around him and the startled look on his face. She'd looked at him that day and none of those things had registered beyond the fact that she'd had to get the kids to safety, but now it all came rushing at her like a runaway dump truck.

Then she recalled the old man who'd died attempting to protect the children…and the niece who'd trusted the wrong man and paid the ultimate price.

But above all else she thought about Braddock and how he'd sacrificed himself for her. She would likely be dead now if he hadn't taken the decision away from her. He had known, as she did even if she didn't want to admit it, that she wouldn't be able to hold out under interrogation like he could. She didn't have the right training.

Truth was…she was scared to death.

For all the bluster and determination to have her revenge against Sloan, she was terrified that she couldn't help Braddock. That these bastards would somehow manage to find the children and all those people who had died would be for nothing.

The trembling started deep inside her. She tried to control it, but that wasn't happening.

"You okay?" Amy asked quietly.

She scooted closer to Gabrielle. Her voice sounded rusty. Gabrielle wasn't sure if that was from yelling or just from being gagged. Combine all that with the need to barely whisper and the result was pretty much a croak.

"Yeah," Gabrielle lied. "You?"

"I've been better." She laughed softly but the sound held no humor. "My first real field assignment and I get myself captured."

Gabrielle looked at the woman through the darkness. She couldn't see anything except a shadowy outline but she'd kind of gotten used to that in that frigging cave.

"You're doing great." Gabrielle doubted her opinion meant that much to the other woman but she had to speak her mind. She hadn't gotten a good look at Amy but from what Gabrielle could tell she'd taken a hell of a beating.

The tension throbbed between them for a minute or so. It didn't take a mind reader to know what she was thinking. She and Gabrielle weren't on the same side in this, at least not technically.

"In a way, I suppose," Amy offered, "your coming down here was a sort of blessing in disguise."

Gabrielle didn't laugh outright for fear the guys up front would hear them, but she did make a soft scoffing sound. "That's one way to look at it."

"If," Amy went on, "you hadn't come after Sloan, no one would have known what was going on with the boys until it was too late."

Gabrielle had considered that. If she hadn't shown up when she had…well, she didn't know what would have happened but it couldn't have been good.

"Sloan will owe you a great debt."

Anger flared but Gabrielle kept it to herself. She didn't want to talk about Sloan right now. She didn't even want to think about him. She hadn't done anything for him, she'd done what she did for the children.

"We need a plan for rescuing Braddock," she said, shifting the conversation to the matter at hand.

"Right," Amy agreed.

Gabrielle stretched out her shoulders and neck and waited for Amy to suggest a tactic. She'd been at the Colby Agency far longer than Gabrielle, had probably listened to the other investigators numerous times.

"From what I picked up on," Amy went on, "in the conversations I overheard, these guys work for some big-time slave trader."

Gabrielle and Braddock had talked about that but this seemed like a hell of a lot of trouble just to nab two kids. "They've gone to an awful lot of trouble for two kids," she said, giving voice to the thought. "The search party alone involved enough men to launch a small war." She shook her head. "Doesn't make sense to me."

"You're right," Amy explained. "Apparently, Sloan has been doing a little digging into the increasing disappearances of tourists and temporary residents. You know, the folks who come down here to live for a couple years while overseeing or participating in some business development."

Gabrielle had lived in Texas most of her life. She was very well aware of the growing slave trade and kidnap-ransom business down here. "You think someone hired Sloan to do a little investigating."

"I don't know. Maybe he simply discovered something that led him to do a little investigating on his own. Whatever the case, he got someone's attention and they decided the best way to get him off their back was to exterminate him and his family. From what little I know, abduction is big business down here."

She was right about that. Bastards. Gabrielle wondered how people like that lived with themselves. No conscience.

The story Braddock had told her about Angel…her father…killing Sloan's wife and taking his son zinged into her consciousness.

That couldn't be right.

Just somebody's tale to warp the truth.

"They'll torture Braddock in hopes of extracting the whereabouts of the children from him," Gabrielle said more to herself than to the other woman.

"For sure," Amy agreed. "I'm just guessing here, but I'll bet they've waited for this opportunity when Sloan would be out of town. They likely had one of their men get close to Pablo's niece to keep tabs on Sloan. They want to hurt the children first to hurt him. Maybe to learn exactly what he knows and if he's told anyone else."

Gabrielle's stomach churned. How could they do that? Harm children. It felt impossible that anyone could be so heartless.

"Braddock won't cave." Gabrielle knew this if she knew nothing else at all. Braddock would not give up the location of the children.

"No. He'll die first."

Emotions she couldn't fully label roared through Gabrielle. Amy was right. He would die today or tonight. As soon as these scumbags realized he wasn't going to talk, he would die.

"I can't let that happen," Gabrielle said firmly. She would not let it happen.

"If they suspect you're here, you'll lose your leverage," Amy whispered. "I think they believe you're dead. From what I overheard they weren't worried about you once they found A.J."

"They'll know I'm alive after I help you escape," Gabrielle countered. The two men up front would have to die and the others would guess the reason; clearly they weren't stupid, just evil.

"That's why I have to stay."

That startling realization shuddered through Gabrielle. Amy was right. To maintain the element of surprise they had to believe that Gabrielle was out of the picture, no threat to their evil scheme.

"They're taking me to the boss," Amy murmured. "To the compound."

Gabrielle had heard that reference herself. "Yeah, I heard them say something about a compound."

"They've probably taken A.J. there, too. Once these two have dragged me out of the van—and I won't make it easy—you'll have some time to make your move."

"Braddock told me to call Victoria," she said, remembering his final instructions to her.

"That wouldn't hurt," Amy allowed, "but the truth is, there might not be enough time for Victoria to get help to us. You may have to do something on your own."

Gabrielle licked her lips thoughtfully. "I can do that."

The beginnings of a plan started to form, but she would need help.

"Let's start with tying you back up," Gabrielle suggested.

Amy nodded.

"Wait." Gabrielle reached into her sock and retrieved the .38. "Can we hide this somewhere on you so you'll be armed?" She took Amy's hand and placed the weapon on her palm.

"Yeah…how about in my sock?"

Gabrielle smiled. Great minds obviously thought alike. "Perfect."

When Amy had hidden the gun away, Gabrielle reassembled her bonds but was careful to leave things so that Amy could work herself loose if the opportunity presented itself.

"I'll hide under the tarp," Gabrielle said, turning over the only option in her head. It stunk like hell but she didn't see any other alternative.

"I think…there's already somebody under there." She sucked in a shaky breath. "Whoever he was, he showed up at Sloan's house at the wrong time."

Hefting her shoulder bag onto her back, Gabrielle crawled on her hands and knees to the pile of material that was the tarp. She felt around for any hard bulges. Sure enough she found a lump. The lump was indeed human, but without any light there was no way to identify the guy.

"I guess we can share the tarp," Gabrielle muttered. "If you give them enough trouble it'll take 'em both to drag you out of here and then they'll have to come back for the body if that's part of their plan. And I'll be long gone."

"They might not be in a hurry to move the body," Amy considered out loud, "but you need to be prepared for that possibility."

"Yeah." Gabrielle would hide behind the body and hope like hell her plan worked.

"I guess you'd better put the gag back into place. They could reach their destination anytime."

Gabrielle felt around for the piece of duct tape.

As she started to press one side against Amy's cheek, she said, "Just so you know, Victoria understands that you have extenuating circumstances. She believes in you, Gabrielle. We all do."

For three beats Gabrielle couldn't react or continue with taping the woman's mouth shut. Her fingers trembled and she felt oddly bereft.

When she'd regained her composure, she pressed the tape into place without responding. What could she say? Some part of her appreciated that a woman like

Victoria had that much faith in her, but that didn't change the facts.

Gabrielle had come here on a mission. Her ultimate intentions had not changed.

A.J. LAY ON THE stone floor. His body throbbed with pain. He prayed he would reach that plateau soon where he felt nothing at all.

He'd lost a lot of blood. Felt weak. Thankfully the bullet hadn't hit anything vital, just tore through flesh and muscle, leaving him leaking a steady flow of blood. He thought the leak had slowed a little now but couldn't be sure since moving to take a look was out of the question. If he moved, a whole barrage of pain would be set off.

He'd been kicked until he'd lost consciousness. Then when he'd arrived at the main compound of these bastards they'd started in using him as a punching bag until he'd blacked out again.

His eyes were pretty much swollen shut and his lips were cracked open. He had at least one fractured rib and various other bruises and abrasions. Otherwise he was unharmed.

The thought almost made him laugh. Almost.

He couldn't be certain just yet who the main man running this operation was, but he thought one of the two who'd stood back and watched his last beating might be the head honcho. Not that the information would do A.J. any good. He was just curious.

The primary objective for these scumbags was to extract the location of the children. They wanted those kids bad.

He closed his eyes and wished for sleep and the relief from pain it would bring. But the adrenaline flowing through his body, prompted by the pain, wouldn't permit that much needed respite.

If he couldn't lose himself to sleep maybe he could go for a waking fantasy. Shouldn't be that hard. All he had to do was think about Gabrielle.

She was safe. He knew it. She was too strong and too capable to get caught considering the out he'd given her.

He admired the way she showed her determination in the field. She'd risked everything to help those kids. She'd stuck right with him when it would have been in her best interest to cut out. To save herself and to hell with him or the kids.

And that wasn't even counting the way his body had responded to hers in that hole while they'd lain there all those hours. He'd almost lost his mind, had come close to losing his dignity, as well.

She made him want to risk whatever the future held. She made him want more from life.

It was just a dream. A fantasy. He couldn't put anyone's, especially not Gabrielle's, heart on the line. He couldn't promise her next year or even next week. His health was too uncertain.

But he could fantasize about what it would be like to make love to her. To have her as a part of his life. Not just for a few days but for the long haul.

His eyes closed and he thought of how it would feel for them to be lying together skin to skin…the soft swells and valleys of her body molding to his hard contours. She would be an ambitious lover, he was certain. Her arms around him and her mouth devouring his. That would be heaven. She'd wanted to take that one kiss they'd shared a lot deeper. He'd felt her offering more…inviting him in fully. Maybe he should have followed her lead…let whatever would be happen. Then he wouldn't be lying here regretting not knowing her that way.

The creak of the door warned him someone was coming. A.J. tucked his dreams away and braced himself for what was to come. More torture. Maybe something more creative this time. The punches and kicking were getting old. Surely these guys had a better bag of tricks.

An order, sharply issued in Spanish, was made for the prisoner to be restrained in a different manner. A.J. didn't fully understand the swiftly doled out orders.

A.J. pried his swollen eyes open just enough to see through the meager slits as two men, one on either side of him, tugged him to his feet. He swallowed the groan of pain that shuddered through him on the heels of the misery the movement initiated.

His arms were secured tightly above his head and he was left to hang there like a side of beef. His feet were on the ground but there was no way in his current condition that he could hold up his weight. His shirt and T-shirt had been ripped from him hours ago. He didn't have to look down to know his chest was likely black and blue and skinned here and there. Not to mention the bullet hole low on his side.

"Mr. Braddock," a voice said, one he hadn't heard before, "your resistance is becoming tedious."

A.J. worked hard at getting his eyes open far enough and his face angled in the right direction to see the person addressing him. Tall. Definitely Hispanic. Wore a suit for the occasion. Expensive suit. Classy shoes. He'd seen him before, standing back watching the show. So A.J.'d been right, this was the top dog.

"Sorry I'm boring you, you piece of dirt," A.J. muttered, his lips stinging with the effort.

The man swept the lapels of his elegant suit aside and braced his hands on his hips. Rings glittered from several fingers. He looked as if he hadn't done a hard day's work in his life. Appeared to be about thirty-five and well-manicured. He reeked of money.

"I don't want to kill you, Mr. Braddock." The man smiled. Nice teeth, too. Probably spent megabucks keeping them all shiny and bright white. "At least not yet. I want the location of the children."

"I want a vacation," A.J. snapped back, "but, hey, we don't always get what we want."

His meticulously maintained face hardened. "My friends here want to utilize another technique for learning the truth from you."

The squeak of wheels turning called A.J.'s attention toward the steel cart rolling toward him. The lowlife pushing the cart grinned widely at A.J.'s sudden interest.

The cart held an array of goods, most of which A.J. recognized. A battery for producing a charge. A set of something similar to jumper cables for jump-starting a car. Only these cables had been modified on one end. The modifications allowed for paddles that could be pressed to human flesh and which could conduct an electrical charge that would prove immensely painful but wouldn't induce death by stopping the heart.

"I'm inclined to believe," the well-dressed bastard continued, "that additional torture is not necessary."

A.J. looked from the suit to the grinning idiot and back. "I don't have any other plans for the afternoon."

The suit nodded to his less well-groomed cohort. "In that case, I'll leave you to the games." He started to turn away but then shifted back to face A.J. "When I return, I'll bring along your friend. Perhaps you'll be more co-operative in her company."

Fear throttled through A.J. Had they caught Gabrielle? He'd hoped she would get away.

His attention was momentarily distracted by the flying sparks generated by rubbing the two paddles together.

Well, at least it would be a change from the routine so far. He steeled himself for the agony to come and focused on an image of Gabrielle. If he were lucky the electrical current would stop his heart and he wouldn't have to watch her tortured.

But that would be the easy way out.

If she had been caught then he had to figure out a way to get loose so he could help her.

He couldn't let her go through anything like this.

As PROMISED, Amy struggled, whipping her body like a bow in the hands of the two men. They swore, labored to get her under control so she could be carried to wherever they intended to take her.

Gabrielle had positioned herself where she could see under the edge of the tarp beyond the stiff taking up space in front of her. The smell was nearly intolerable. Knowing hers as well as Amy's and Braddock's lives depended upon her keeping quiet was all that stalled the instinctive need to gag repeatedly.

Amy wiggled, moaned and groaned and threw her head back. The latter resulted in a couple of head butts with her captors. Curses and threats punctuated the men's efforts to get her under control. Gabrielle had to give the other woman credit, she was doing a stellar job of making their lives miserable for the moment.

Finally they gave up on any real control and dragged her away, their full attention required for the task.

Gabrielle scrambled out from under the tarp. She carefully re-covered the stiff, on second thought taking a moment to see if she recognized him. Male, Hispanic. She hadn't seen him before, she was certain.

She glanced out the rear van doors, didn't see anyone. She decided to take a chance and check the guy for ID. A leather wallet held official credentials. Detective Hernando Cervantes. Cop. Damn.

Apparently these guys weren't afraid of anyone, not even the police.

Gabrielle eased to the rear doors, still standing open the way the two jerks had left them, and stole a peek outside. A compound was definitely the right way to describe the location.

Like Sloan's property, the whole place was protected by a high wall of about ten or twelve feet. Several buildings, none as nice as Sloan's house, occupied the property. One looked like a three-story residence. All appeared to be constructed of stone and stucco.

She hadn't seen any guards as of yet, but that didn't mean there weren't plenty around.

Holding her breath, she slipped out of the van and headed for the nearest cover, a small building near the wall.

She flattened against the side of the building and surveyed the area first left then right.

The sun beat down on the stone walls, drives and walkways, forcing the heat to rise as if coming from a preheated oven. Or hell.

Her heart prematurely contracted when two men, both armed, strolled around the corner of one of the larger buildings. The two spoke, too low for her to make out the dialogue, and laughed as they continued across the open courtyard.

She counted six buildings. Staying put and biding her time, she observed more than a dozen men moving around on the property. All were well-armed and physically fit-looking.

No way she could take more than two of them unless she got really lucky.

From what she could tell, the largest of the buildings was a house. Two other buildings were either guard shacks or places where business was conducted. A lot of ground to cover and no backup.

She couldn't do this alone.

Problem was, she didn't know a soul in Mexico except Sloan and she didn't actually know him, not to mention he was out of the country.

As Amy had said, there wasn't time for help to get here from the Colby Agency. Though the men back at the house had mentioned some new arrivals at a private airfield, Gabrielle had no way of knowing who they were talking about.

There was a dead cop in the back of the van she'd

ridden in, which pretty much made the police useless. Who knew if they would even believe her much less have the guts to come back here prepared to fight?

What she needed was a miracle.

First thing she had to do was to get out of here and make a call. There was one person she could ask for advice.

He might not be able to help her, but he'd been in the PI business longer than her; maybe he would have some advice at the very least.

She waited until the coast was clear, then she headed for the wall. There had to be a gate somewhere. The question was, could she get past the guards that would most likely be posted there?

She wouldn't know until she tried.

Two gates. One main front entrance, one less over-powering side entrance. She opted for the latter.

A ride out would be nice since she didn't have any idea where she was. She could see buildings beyond the wall, which made her think she might be in a larger city.

She didn't recognize any of the architectural land-marks. An ancient-looking, pink quarry-stone cathe-dral. Towering stucco buildings. But nothing familiar to her. She had never traveled in Mexico before and whatever she'd studied about it in school was long gone from her memory.

The guard shack was integrated into the gate on one side. The best she could hope for was to get out whenever a vehicle exited by using the vehicle for cover.

She hunkered in the shrubbery near the gate to wait for an opportunity.

Luck appeared to be on her side for once and she didn't have to wait long. A black SUV rolled up to the gate. The driver and the guard in the shack chatted while the gate slowly arched open.

Gabrielle held her breath and emerged from her hiding place. She eased up alongside the SUV and stayed crouched below the level of the windows to prevent being seen. She hoped like hell no one in the house happened to be looking out a window just then and spotted her.

As the SUV rolled forward through the gate, she jogged alongside it, careful to stay next to the rear passenger side tire in the blind spot so she wouldn't be seen by the driver via his mirrors.

Once beyond the gate, she flatted against the exterior of the wall. When the gate had closed and the SUV was out of sight, she dared to move.

The compound sat on the edge of a town. No, not a town. A city. As she looked beyond the three- and four-story buildings on the surrounding streets, she could see a massive city sprawled over the landscape. The architecture was magnificent.

Finally she spotted a sign. Chihuahua.

Okay, at least she knew where she was.

All she needed now was a phone.

She walked along the street, considered the options. Would anyone allow her to use the phone? And even if someone let her use the phone, would the long-distance service be like that of the U.S.?

No, she decided. What she needed were American tourists. That would require she get deeper into the city.

Gabrielle hailed the next driver who passed and in her best broken Spanish offered him twenty bucks in American money to take her to the nearest tourist hangout.

The driver was a smart guy. He took Gabrielle to a large open air market. Very popular with the American tourists, he assured her. She gave him his money and thanked him profusely. He didn't comment on her haggard and dirty appearance.

Gabrielle immersed herself in the crowd of tourists. She pretended to consider the goods being sold but her attention had zeroed in on two Americans who looked particularly well-to-do. Fancy dressers. The woman carried a designer handbag that cost more than two months' rent back at Gabrielle's Chicago apartment.

The man wore his cell phone in a holster on his belt.

That was Gabrielle's target.

She needed that phone.

When the couple stopped at a table loaded with Mexican pottery, Gabrielle saw her chance. She strolled over, pretended to trip and fall into the man, who in turn knocked his wife forward. Pottery shattered on the cobblestone. The man hawking the goods scrambled to save his stock.

"I'm so sorry," Gabrielle cried, steadying herself by holding on to the man.

"You all right?" he asked as he helped her to regain her footing.

"You should watch where you're going," his female companion snapped as she righted herself.

"Sorry," Gabrielle said again as she backed away a step. She shrugged at the vendor. "Sorry."

He swore at her in Spanish and made a sweeping motion with his hands as if he wanted her to get away from his table. Gabrielle was happy to oblige. She already had what she needed.

She moved quickly away from the couple. She wanted to get as far away as possible before the man realized his cell phone was missing.

Then she found a quiet place and opened the phone. She smiled. Latest technology. Fully charged. Oh, yeah. This was exactly what she'd needed.

She entered the number for Todd Thompson's cell phone.

"Thompson."

Gabrielle moistened her lips and took a steadying breath. "Thompson, I need your help."

"Gabrielle? Where the hell are you? What have you gotten yourself into?"

"Look, Thompson, I don't have time to explain. I need your help."

Silence. Gabrielle closed her eyes and for the second time in her adult life, she prayed.

"What do you need?"

Emotion burned her eyes and she promised God she would pay him back for this. "I don't have time to explain all the details, but the bad guys have Braddock and Amy. They're both dead if I can't break them out."

"I should let Victoria know," he said, tension rising in his voice.

"In a minute. Right now I need you to access the system and tell me what supply assets in Chihuahua can be relied on."

"You're in Chihuahua?"

"Yeah. Look, Thompson, you have to hurry or it'll be too late."

"Okay, okay." She could hear him pecking at the keys of his office computer. "What type of assets do you need?"

Gabrielle had thought about that. Hoping to find backup was too risky. There was no way to know who she could count on and who she couldn't. Besides, she had Braddock and Amy, all she needed was enough of a distraction to get them freed and the three of them could fight their way out if necessary. But that scenario depended upon her being able to create a big enough diversion to keep all those guards busy.

Not a problem. She'd come up with a workable plan. All she needed was the right supplies.

"Nothing complicated," she assured him. "I just need to blow something up."

Chapter Thirteen

Gabrielle looked at the building then at the address just to make sure she had it right.

Yep. Man, talk about a pigsty. The terra-cotta stucco had faded to something along the lines of a nasty orangey beige. Several of the windows were boarded over. Abandoned junk lay around outside. Not exactly an upscale address.

The weight of her 9 mm in her shoulder bag gave her some amount of comfort but even she, and she could be pretty cocky, recognized this meeting could go badly.

Still, she didn't have time to do any better. This was it. She looked at the clock on the cell phone she'd stolen. An hour had passed since she'd left Amy at that compound. Every minute could be Braddock's as well as Amy's last. The cell phone had started to ring soon after she'd lifted it, so she'd set the ringer style to silent.

Thompson was certain about this point of contact.

Well, as certain as he could be considering he'd never met the guy. This was a Colby Agency asset. Last recorded contact, three years ago.

Hell, the guy could be dead, for all Gabrielle knew.

But he was the only contact she had.

And since she had very little cash with her, she was going to have to wing it on that, as well.

Oh well, if she died today it wasn't likely a couple more infractions were going to make or break her destiny.

She walked up to the front entrance of the building, didn't slow down until she'd marched right through the door. Inside the condition was about the same: falling apart. The beige-brown stuff on the floor might have once been carpet, but she couldn't be sure.

The smell, well it was better than the van, but that wasn't saying much considering there had been a dead man along for the ride.

Gabrielle shuddered. A dead detective. Not a good sign for things to come.

The enemy wasn't afraid of the local authorities. That much was clear.

"You lost, lady?" The man who greeted her looked anything but happy to have company. His face was too thin, his nose too long, and the beady eyes didn't help his overall lack of appeal. He did dress well though. Pleated slacks, button-down shirt with a tie hanging loose around his neck.

The skinny guy's accent was thick but at least he spoke English. Considering how bad Gabrielle's Spanish was, that would make this meeting a lot easier.

"I'm here to see Chico."

The man's gaze narrowed. "I don't know any Chico."

Damn. Gabrielle didn't want him to be dead or otherwise out of business.

"That's too bad. Sloan sent me to see him."

The mention of Sloan's name altered the man's entire demeanor. Maybe Sloan was good for something besides killing, after all. She booted the thought out of her mind. She couldn't let anything distract her right now.

"Maybe you're talking about Vega. Some people call him Chico." He inclined his head knowingly. "Like your friend Sloan."

He didn't have to know Sloan was her enemy. "That must be him." She pushed a smile into place. "Is he in?"

The guy stood. "Of course he's in, where else would he be?"

Gabrielle didn't bother with a response. She figured it was a rhetorical question.

She followed the skinny guy deeper into the building. The corridor he took wasn't completely dark, but it was too dimly lit for her comfort. Adrenaline blasted through her veins as she kept telling herself over and over that she could do this. She'd met people in prison who reminded her of this guy. Women who would do just about anything for a pack of cigarettes. Only they hadn't dressed as well.

When they neared the back of the building he stopped at a closed door and knocked. It opened instantly, as if someone had been waiting on the other side to do nothing but open the door.

A big guy stood in the opening. "Yeah?"

"He's got a visitor," the skinny guy said.

Gabrielle took a long, deep breath and ordered herself to calm. She could do this, she repeated silently.

The big guy backed out of the doorway and the skinny one gestured for her to go in.

Gabrielle didn't smile at him. She doubted if people who shopped here did much smiling.

The door closed behind her as soon as she'd cleared it. She didn't have to look back to know the big guy now blocked it. A bodyguard, she decided.

The man behind the desk on the far side of the room was deep into a telephone conversation. In Spanish, of course. She listened for Sloan's name but didn't hear it. She wasn't prepared for him to check out her story, wouldn't matter most likely. Sloan was out of the country. Pablo was dead. There was no one to answer the phone at his place.

She didn't sit, just stood a few feet away from his desk and waited.

Maybe she should sit, she considered when the conversation lagged on.

Nah. She didn't want to get comfortable. She had a request. As soon as she'd made it and got what she needed, she was out of here.

His desktop looked neat and orderly surprisingly enough. The room itself wasn't very different from most offices belonging to businessmen who operated in low-rent areas. Maybe this wouldn't be as complicated as she'd feared.

The click of the receiver coming to rest in the cradle jerked her attention back to the desk and the man, Chico or Vega.

"So." He propped his elbows on his desk and steepled his fingers. "Sloan sent you to me, did he?"

Okay. This was where things could get sticky.

"Actually," she said, going with her first instinct, "Sloan said I should forget the whole thing, but I can't do that."

He eyed her speculatively for ten or so seconds. She stopped counting at ten.

"What can't you forget, *señora?*"

"Those bastards have my man," she said, going with her first instinct, no holds barred. "I want him back. I can't do it by myself."

"There are many bastards in this city," he countered. "Who has taken your man?"

Now came the moment of truth. She didn't know the boss's name so she gave Chico/Vega the address of the compound.

His eyebrows shot up his forehead. "Do you under-stand who you're dealing with? These people would as soon kill you as look at you." His gaze roved the length of her and back. "Even one so inspiring to look at."

She swallowed hard, tried not to let her nervousness show. "Not if I kill them first."

He laughed, just one brief sound of amusement. "How do you expect to do this? You said you have no help. I must warn you that it appears you are very much in over your head."

Yeah, yeah, she'd heard that from Thompson, too.

"I know exactly how deep I'm in," she said crisply, ensuring the determination in her eyes arrowed straight into his. "And I know what I have to do."

He nodded. "Again, I ask, how do you plan to do this thing you must?"

"I need explosives." She shrugged. "C-4, dyna-mite, whatever."

A smile played about one corner of his mouth. "You plan to blow them up, is that it, *señora*?"

"That's about the size of it," she returned without hesitation.

"My, my," he said, "fireworks and it is well past the festival."

"That's right," she agreed. Lots of fireworks.

"Anything else?"

Her heart skipped a beat. Did this mean he was going to help her? "A couple of 9 mm clips and ammo for a .38 automatic." She might as well get some extra ammo while she was at it. If Amy had managed to get in with the weapon still in her sock she would need ammo, too.

"And how would you be paying for this merchandise?"

Gabrielle's enthusiasm fizzled a little. One more sticking point.

"Sloan said he had a tab with you," she offered. She hadn't meant for the statement to come out sounding so hopeful and downright desperate.

"This is true," he agreed with a nod. "But you, *señora,* do not."

Damn.

Okay, she was running out of time here.

"There must be some way we can work this out," she suggested. She knew how it sounded and as much as she hated to admit it, she meant it exactly the way it sounded.

She had to do whatever it took.

Her stomach roiled at the idea.

Then inspiration struck. "But then," she countered, "I'm not sure how Sloan would take it if he discovered you'd taken advantage of me. We're cousins, you know." She was definitely going to hell. No question.

Those dark eyes narrowed to mere slits as he regarded her challenge.

Gabrielle held her breath. Did a little more of that praying she'd done today. She needed these supplies.

She needed to get out of here in a hurry. For once she needed fate to be on her side.

"I'm certain Sloan will be happy to settle your debt. Perhaps I will call him to confirm your assertions."

A surge of uncertainty made her feel faint but she refused to give in to the weakness. "Do what you've gotta do, pal, just don't waste any time. Time is my enemy."

Chico's gaze settled heavily onto hers. "*Señora*, it would appear the devil himself is your enemy."

She supposed that meant that he knew the owner of the property she planned to blow up. Considering the bastard who'd abducted her friends and his determination to harm small children she'd say he was the devil himself, as well.

GABRIELLE LEFT the faded, rundown stucco building with enough C-4 in her shoulder bag to blow up two city blocks. She had four 9 mm clips and ammo for the .38.

She stayed on her toes. Now would not be the time to get mugged.

The taxi ride back to the compound on the fringes of the west side of the city took far longer than she would have liked. She realized it was more her impatience than anything else. But she couldn't bear the thought that Braddock and Amy might be dying right now.

Her throat went bone dry. She didn't know Amy that well but she didn't deserve this. And Braddock, well, he'd gotten under Gabrielle's skin and she couldn't think of anything but him.

If he died because of her...

This situation wasn't entirely her fault. The people holding Braddock had a vendetta against Sloan. Join the crowd, she mused. Still, Braddock wouldn't even have been in Mexico if he hadn't come for her. That made his situation all her fault.

She moistened her lips and sucked in a heavy breath. Her chest hurt. Her head hurt. Her whole body hurt for that matter.

And there was still the business with Sloan.

Gabrielle closed her eyes and tried to block the questions that filtered through her mind when she thought of Sloan now. She didn't want to believe what Braddock had told her about her father. That would make everything she'd believed her entire life a lie. All of it couldn't be lies. Surely her mother wouldn't have done that to her.

No. She understood the situation perfectly. Sloan's friends wanted to believe the best in him just as her mother had believed the best in Gabrielle's father.

The difference was that Sloan was alive and Gabrielle's father was dead. He couldn't tell his side of things and Sloan had killed him.

She relaxed her arms. *Don't be squeezing the C-4,* she reminded.

Staying focused was absolutely essential right now.

Chico had given her a quick block of instruction on the use of the C-4. She let him. She'd seen it before and knew a little bit about it, but she had to admit that his instructions were much clearer than the lowlifes's up in Montana who'd trained her on weaponry.

Her plan was simple. She would get back inside the gate. Then she would covertly move from building to building and pray she didn't get caught. She would verify the location of Amy and Braddock, then, one by one, since she only had one very simple, single channel remote, she would blow up a section of a building. Hopefully the unexpected attack would distract those holding Braddock and Amy and she could free them. During the resulting turmoil the three of them would escape.

Sounded easy enough.

"Here, *señora?*"

The driver's question snapped her out of her troubling thoughts. She looked around, noted the street. "Yes, this is good." She paid the fare and climbed out, careful not to bump her bag.

She walked quickly along the cobblestone alleyway until she reached the far side of the block. She waited in the shadows of the alleyway and studied the front gate of the compound.

Two guards. One at the side gate, one at the front. At least two dozen men roaming around inside.

This wasn't going to be easy.

But she had to try.

She couldn't let Amy or Braddock die.

Some cruel brain cell ushered forth the memory of that one kiss she and Braddock had shared. She so desperately wanted more from him. She hadn't wanted any man to touch her that way in a very long time. She'd been too caught up in her determination to make Sloan pay and to survive prison.

She'd had several boyfriends in high school, even a couple afterward. But no one had ever made her want more than a physically exhausting tangle beneath the sheets until Braddock. He made her want to explore a *relationship*.

Unbelievable.

Her mother had warned her over and over how dangerous it was to give a guy that much control.

But there was no stopping the way she felt. She wanted to know Braddock on every possible level.

The chances of that happening were slim to none. He was being tortured, if he wasn't dead already, and she was standing here with enough explosives to blow herself to smithereens.

A hell of a time for her to realize she wanted more out of life.

A.J. DRIFTED in and out of consciousness.

He told himself to stay awake but he just couldn't do it.

The shock torture had drained the last of his energy. He was hanging on by a thread and the fact that his hands were still secured high above his head.

He didn't have much confidence he'd survive

another round. His persecutors had rubbed salt into his bullet wound and gouged around until he'd passed out when the electrical torture hadn't done the trick.

His mouth and throat felt as dry as sandpaper. He would give most anything for a drink of water.

…and to see Gabrielle one last time.

He might just be able to die happy if he knew she was all right. He licked his lips and summoned the memory of her taste. God he'd wanted to hold her like that and never let go. Why the hell hadn't he asked her out before?

They'd worked together for a while before she'd taken off after Sloan. Maybe if he'd gotten to know her, he could have headed this off. Could have helped her see how wrong she was. But then, if she hadn't come after Sloan, no one would have been there to help the children.

A.J. hadn't ever really believed in fate. He'd believed in determination and grit. If a man wanted something, he had to make it happen. But this whole thing felt exactly like fate.

"Mr. Braddock."

A.J. forced his swollen eyes open as far as possible and watched as the man whose name he didn't know approached him. This guy hadn't actually done any of the torture himself. He was the boss the others referred to. He just gave the orders.

Sick bastard.

"My patience with you grows thin," he said, his sneer making an already ugly mug even uglier.

"Well," A.J. said with a pained laugh, "I have to tell ya, I'm not exactly having a ball myself."

He put his face in A.J.'s. "Tell me where the children are and we'll end this now. Save yourself any more discomfort, you fool. Tell me where they are!"

"No way," A.J. shot back. "Go ahead and do whatever you feel the need to do. I ain't talking, *jefe*," he added with all the hostility he could marshal.

The man stepped back. "Bring in the woman."

A.J.'s heart thumped hard. For the first time since they'd captured him, panic clawed at his throat. He'd yearned to see Gabrielle again…but not like this. When they'd threatened to bring in his friend earlier and hadn't, he'd assumed they were bluffing.

This was the one thing he wasn't sure he could endure.

By the time the two guards came in dragging a female between them his chest felt ready to explode.

Long dark hair.

Oh, God.

She was jerked upright and his gaze landed on her face.

Not Gabrielle.

His relief was short-lived. Amy. Amy Calhoun.

"Let her go," he roared, fury obliterating all other emotion.

"I'm afraid that's quite impossible, Mr. Braddock. You see, she is part of our Plan B to acquire your cooperation."

One of the guards grabbed her by the hair and snapped her head back. Amy cried out.

"Shall we continue, Mr. Braddock?"

A.J. knew he had to do something. He couldn't let them hurt Amy.

But a part of him understood that they were both dead no matter what he did or said.

His gaze met Amy's across the desolate space and he knew she fully comprehended the situation.

They were both dead.

With that one look she telegraphed her own determination to him…. *Don't give in….*

GABRIELLE WAITED as close to the side entry gate as she dared. The guard was busy talking on his cell phone, but so far no one had come in or out of the compound, allowing her no opportunity to get in.

She couldn't keep waiting for a break…she was going to have to make one.

Her hiding place didn't offer much in the way of options. She was out of sight but not much else.

She needed to be closer…she needed a way in without attracting attention to herself.

Might as well call it what it was. She needed that miracle she'd been wishing for.

She could shoot the guard and go in. But that would cost her the element of surprise as well as send a huge signal to the rest of the psychos hanging around the compound that she had arrived.

Okay. Maybe there was something she could do.

She crouched and opened her shoulder bag. She carefully picked through the goods until she located the utility knife Chico'd given her for resizing the C-4 if necessary.

If she cut her jeans really short and tied her T-shirt under her breasts, maybe she could distract the guard and get in that way.

The roar of vehicles approaching on the street from her right yanked Gabrielle's attention back to the gate.

She dropped the knife into the bag and hefted it up and onto her shoulder. Deciding that being prepared was preferable to comfort, she jammed her 9 mm into the waistband of her khakis, right next to her bellybutton, the way Braddock had.

Focus, she ordered. Three vehicles—two cars and an SUV—had stopped at the side gate.

Gabrielle's heart rate climbed dramatically as she watched the guard step outside his shack to chat with the driver of the first car.

She squinted, tried to get a look at the passengers in the vehicles. Two in the first one. Only two...no, three in the second one, then only a driver in the SUV.

Damn. Just what she needed. Additional manpower.

She forked her fingers through her hair and decided it was now or never. All she had to do was to slip in behind the SUV, crouch and then move through the gate alongside it. If she stayed in the blind spot on the passenger side, the driver wouldn't see her in the mirror and the guard wouldn't be able to see her since she'd be on the opposite side of the vehicle.

It had worked once before.

At this point she was pretty much desperate.

She was running out of time and her options were sorely limited.

Braddock or Amy or both could be dead by now. She couldn't risk wasting any more time.

This was it.

She took a deep, fortifying breath and steeled herself to run the short distance between her position and the rear of the SUV.

On the count of three, she told herself as she surveyed the narrow street for anyone who might see her when she stepped away from her cover. She couldn't get caught or the game would be over and they would all be losers.

"I wouldn't do that if I were you."

She whipped around, her weapon leveled on the sound of the voice behind her.

Her breath evacuated her lungs in a mad rush as her eyes identified the man who'd stolen up behind her with the same quiet danger as smoke from a smoldering fire.

Extraordinarily intense blue eyes…unruly, sandy-blond hair…ruggedly handsome face.

Trevor Sloan.

She had memorized every damned detail of what he looked like years ago…had dreamed about this day every waking moment for months and months…

He stood barely three feet from her.

Her weapon was leveled center chest.

All she had to do was to pull the trigger and it would be done.

Chapter Fourteen

"I know who you are."

The words reverberated through Gabrielle and suddenly her body was quaking, as if the words had set off some chain reaction.

"The way I see it, we can settle this now or we can go in there and help out your friends," he added.

Her palms started to sweat, forcing her to tighten her grip on the butt of her 9 mm.

His gaze never deviated from hers. If the weapon pointed at him worried him, he didn't let it show. He just kept staring at her as if the ball was in her court and she needed to take her serve.

During the trauma-filled moments that followed, Gabrielle considered that if she put her gun away, basically gave up her advantage, he could whip out his weapon and put a bullet in her before she could blink.

Maybe he would kill her, but she couldn't sweat about that just now. She had to get in there and save

Braddock and Amy. Every second she squandered standing here put Braddock that much closer to dead…she swallowed hard…if he wasn't already.

Apprehension pulsing in her veins, she lowered her weapon. "I take it you have a plan?"

He glanced toward the gate that had closed behind the entourage of vehicles. "Let's see what Chico gave us to work with."

Startled that he knew about her negotiations with the less than savory character, she heard herself ask, "How did you know I talked to Chico?" She cringed at how stupid the question was. His explosives contact had obviously called to let him know someone was throwing his name around.

"Let's just say you've been anything but subtle, Miss Jordan, and leave it at that."

Indignation seeped in, overriding the other, more awkward feelings. She started to tell him that he could keep his smart-ass remarks to himself but he didn't give her the chance.

"Whatever your agenda with me, you helped my sons, for that I owe you. I always repay my debts."

That he called Josh his son wasn't lost on her, nor was the concept that he settled his debts.

So this was Sloan, the man of honor, the hero.

The man who'd killed her father.

Hard as it proved, she held back that accusation. "How do we make this happen?"

A grin hitched up one corner of his grim mouth. "Now that's the easy part. You just do what I tell you and we'll get through this alive."

For what it was worth, she believed him.

Sloan didn't go in quietly and covertly, as she'd planned to. Instead he'd slung his arm around her neck and pulled her close as if she were his girlfriend. She resisted at first, but her need to help Braddock and Amy overrode her conflict. Together she and Sloan strolled, and stumbled, over to the guard shack.

The guard promptly ordered them to get lost.

"All I need is a light, man," Sloan said, sounding inebriated and waving a cigarette he'd produced from the pocket in his denim jacket. He shoved his hand through his hair and looked around. "I think we're lost, baby."

More cursing from the guard who didn't want them hanging around.

"All right, all right," Sloan assured him. He waved his arms magnanimously. "Just tell me how to get outta here and we're gone."

The guard stepped out of his small, protective structure and pointed to the right while blustering in broken English which direction they should take.

Sloan moved closer to him as if trying to understand what and where he meant. The guard abruptly slumped forward. Sloan ushered him back into the guard shack and pressed the button that would open the gate.

Still standing with her jaw sagging, realization

finally kicked in as she saw Sloan shove the weapon back into his waistband. Silencer. His weapon was equipped with a silencer. She should have gotten one of those from that ratfink Chico.

As soon as they were inside Sloan closed the gate and snagged the dead guard's walkie-talkie.

Two minutes and Gabrielle was impressed already.

She evicted the thought and reminded herself that this was Sloan…her father's killer. He didn't deserve her admiration, however fleeting.

They stole their way to the closest building. Rows of bunks identified the structure as barracks for the men who served the evil bastard running this operation.

With Gabrielle playing the part of assistant, Sloan planted C-4 in two places in the deserted building.

"Just enough to ensure they'll need to remodel right away," he explained with another of those lopsided smiles.

Two more smaller buildings were rigged for fireworks and the final one besides the main house had been searched before the alarm sounded.

Gabrielle moved up behind Sloan. He'd used two parked SUVs for cover to get closer to the main house.

"Guess that means they found the guard," Gabrielle suggested. Anxiety had tightened like a noose around her neck. They still hadn't found Braddock or Amy. That their presence would now be known made the situation all the more urgent.

"We still have the main house," he said, seemingly

oblivious to her growing panic. "We have to assume he's keeping them there."

Unless they were dead already and he'd disposed of the bodies.

God, why hadn't she moved more quickly? It had been hours since she'd slipped away from here, leaving Amy and Braddock to face certain death. She should have been able to do something…anything.

"We don't have time for that," Sloan said, recognizing her self-deprecation and hauling her attention back to him.

Shouts and the sound of boots running over cobblestone were multiplying all around them. He was right. They had to do this now.

"Let's roll." She was ready. She wanted to take down every one of these scumbags she could. Until there was no one left standing.

She surveyed the rear of the main residence. Armed men were everywhere. No way they could get past them.

"Let's give them something to talk about." Sloan depressed the button on the transmitter and an explosion shook the ground.

The men scattered. Sloan rushed toward the house. Gabrielle stayed right on his heels. The main house was stucco and brick with a typical tiled roof. Huge, bigger than Sloan's maybe. Three floors that sprawled to within a dozen feet of the towering security walls on either side.

The shouting and other buzz of hysteria echoed

around the compound. The distraction had worked like a fight breaking out in the prison yard. No one wanted to miss the possibility of spilled blood or broken bones.

Getting in through the back door of the house without being spotted was a cinch. Avoiding the residents or the armed guerrillas was not.

In the kitchen they hid in the pantry when hurried footsteps echoed in the hall.

Gabrielle's head had started to spin. She steeled herself and refused to give in to the fatigue. She hadn't eaten since the wild potatoes and strawberries. She'd had little or no sleep. And she was so damned confused.

None of this was turning out the way she'd expected.

What happened to her simple plan?

The kids had happened.

Braddock had happened.

And now *him*.

She forced her eyes open and stared at the man through the semidarkness. How could she be hiding in a food closet with her father's killer?

Sloan peered through the crack as he slowly opened the door. "Clear," he muttered.

Chastising herself for being distracted yet again, she made sure she didn't fall behind as she followed him through the kitchen. She couldn't let anything slow down her reactions.

A scream echoed from somewhere deep inside the house. She and Sloan stalled in the middle of the kitchen.

Amy.

Gabrielle didn't have to visually confirm her assumption, she knew it was Amy.

"Basement."

Gabrielle agreed with Sloan's conclusion. The scream had sounded as if it came from beneath them.

"Time for another sideshow."

A second explosion, this one closer, felt as if it shook the foundation of the massive house.

Sloan had explained how to use a single channel transmitter for more than one signal. All one had to do was change the settings. Chico had failed to go over that part with her. Maybe he figured she would never make it this far. He'd probably expected to hear a big bang rather quickly after she'd taken off with the goods he'd charged to Sloan's tab.

Rather than the basement door being in the kitchen, they found it in the mammoth entry hall. One door offered a coat closet while the other opened to a set of stairs that curved and plunged beneath the house.

Sloan paused and listened midway down the steps. The ninety-degree turn would expose them to anyone in the large underground room.

"Shoot them both and let's get out of here."

Terror rocketed inside Gabrielle at the harshly issued order that came from beyond their position.

Before Sloan could stop her, she'd barreled around him and down the final few steps. She was firing off rounds before she hit the stone floor. She rolled for cover and popped off a couple more rounds.

The hissing puffs accompanying Sloan's silenced weapon told her he'd followed suit. He'd taken cover behind a table a few feet away from her concealed position near a stainless steel cart.

The three armed guards went down, but the man in the fancy suit was taking the stairs two at a time.

"I've got him," Sloan shouted at her. "Get them out of here."

It wasn't until he gave the order that she let herself look. Somehow she'd avoided doing that, had focused entirely on taking down the guards.

Amy struggled to her feet. Her blouse was ripped and there was blood, but Gabrielle couldn't tell where it was coming from.

"I'm okay," Amy said shakily. "Just gotta stop this bleeding. Take care of A.J."

Gabrielle's heart practically stopped in her chest when she let her gaze settle fully on Braddock.

Hanging by his arms, which were secured high above his head, he looked unconscious. His head hung against his bare chest.

As Gabrielle hurried toward him, shouted his name, he didn't move.

Her palms flattened on his cool skin and her breath caught harshly when she felt his heart beating.

Thank God. Thank God.

She lifted his face toward hers and another gasp escaped her. His face was grotesquely bruised and swollen.

"Braddock," she whispered, emotion tightening her throat and firing up behind her eyes. "Open your eyes, Braddock." She cleared her throat. "I'm here to save your ass. The least you could do is say thanks."

He tried to open his eyes but that wasn't happening. "'Bout time," he muttered past lips brutally split.

She had to get him loose. Gabrielle dragged a chair over and climbed up on it to cut him loose. He crumpled to the floor.

"Come on, Braddock," she urged, ushering her shoulder under his arm. "Get on your feet. You can lean on me."

He groaned, his body shuddering as she tugged against his weight.

"Hurry." Amy was suddenly on the other side of him, helping to pull him to his feet. "We have to get out of here!"

Between the two of them they managed to get Braddock up the narrow staircase. Gabrielle checked the entry hall before they moved from the safety of the small landing at the top of the stairs.

"We need to stop Fuentes," Braddock muttered.

"Don't try to talk," Gabrielle told him, scared to death there was far more damage than what she could see.

"George Fuentes is the son of a bitch responsible for this slave trade operation," Amy explained as they hurried toward the kitchen.

Gabrielle figured going out the back, the way she and Sloan had come in, would be the best.

"Which one was he?" She assumed he would be the guy in the suit Sloan had taken off after, but she didn't know for sure.

"The bastard in the suit," Amy confirmed.

"Sloan went after him," she said, feeling Braddock's weight dragging more heavily. He was really weak. He wasn't going to make it across the compound.

"There's too many of them." Amy was staring out the rear door.

Gabrielle looked past her. Armed men were running around in circles. Panic had set in completely now. There was no sign of Sloan or the other guy, Fuentes.

"Let's try the front." Gabrielle shifted to head in the other direction but Braddock went down onto his knees, pulling her with him.

"Go without me," he said hoarsely.

"No way." Gabrielle tugged harder. "Get up. We're not leaving without you."

"Come on, A.J.," Amy urged. "You can make it."

Gabrielle didn't realize tears were slipping down her cheeks until the salty taste hit her lips. Dammit. She wasn't going to leave him here like this. She was mad. Why the hell was she crying?

When he still didn't get up, she dropped to her knees and took his face in her hands. "Look, Braddock." He couldn't, of course, but he would understand what she meant. "We have unfinished business. Now move!"

SHE WAS RIGHT…they did have unfinished business. A.J. summoned his strength. Forced his legs to work. He couldn't let his condition handicap Gabrielle and Amy. If they refused to leave him, he had no other choice but to suck it up and make his body obey.

"We're out of here," he mumbled as he pushed upward and began to lurch forward once more. He could barely see through the tiny slits of his swollen eyes.

There wasn't any time to ask how the hell she and Sloan ended up working together. Or how they'd orchestrated the explosions. He was just happy as hell to see her. His chest hurt with the need to hug her or cry or maybe both.

Another thirty seconds and he and Amy would have been history.

By the time they reached the entry hall again his entire body pretty much felt as if it were on fire. Broken ribs and more. Not sure just what, but something that wouldn't let him take in a breath without serious pain.

Gabrielle braced him against the wall near the front door. "Don't move," she instructed.

"Don't worry."

Amy slumped next to him against the wall.

"You okay?"

She nodded.

But he knew she wasn't.

"It's clear." Gabrielle moved back into place beneath his right arm like a human crutch. "But we've gotta get out of here, they're shooting each other out there. If they figure out we're still in here, we're done for."

The sun beat down on him the instant they exited the shade of the veranda. The brightness hurt his eyes. He tried to keep up with Gabrielle's long strides but his legs wouldn't work right.

He was slowing them down.

SHE HAD TO KEEP him moving.

A third explosion rent the air and Gabrielle knew that was a signal from Sloan that he was still alive. She hoped he'd gotten Fuentes. Right now she had her hands full with Braddock.

Shouting to her right warned her that they'd been spotted. She fired twice. One guy hit the ground. She didn't look back. Didn't let her mind dwell on the fact that she'd just killed another man.

Faster. They needed to move faster.

The ragtag group reached the final building on the compound and Gabrielle's anxiety had reached full throttle. Getting through that side gate was the last hurdle. But from her current position she couldn't determine if it was safe to proceed.

Gabrielle braced Braddock against a wall and shoved her 9 mm at Amy. "Shoot anything that moves except me or Sloan."

Amy nodded, her fingers trembling as her right hand wrapped around the butt of the weapon.

"Let me go," Braddock rasped. "I can do that much."

"Forget it. You're practically blind." She didn't give him any time to argue. She ran as fast as she could to the other end of the building.

Flattened against the wall, she took a moment to relish the coolness of the stucco where the fierce Mexican sun couldn't reach.

This was it. The final stretch to freedom. Braddock and Amy were still alive. They were almost in the clear.

She just had to get through this last part.

Drawing in a deep, shuddering breath, Gabrielle leaned past the corner, surveyed the drab landscape between the back of the building and the side gate.

Relief rushed through her.

Clear.

She hurried back to the other end of the building, her heart pumping with anticipation.

Almost out of here.

Almost safe.

"Let's go," she ordered as she skidded to a stop.

She propped herself under Braddock's arm and propelled him toward freedom, down the last stretch and—

Face-to-face with two armed men who rounded the far corner, wild-eyed with fury.

She was suddenly on the ground.

Braddock dove into the two men.

Shots rang out.

Gabrielle scrambled back to her feet.

Braddock and one of the men were rolling on the ground. The other charged Gabrielle.

Amy fired.

The charging man dropped like a rock.

Braddock.

Gabrielle's gaze shifted to the two men scuffling on the ground then to Amy. Amy had swung her aim in their direction, but her hand was shaking so badly…

"Don't shoot," Gabrielle yelled. "You could hit—"

A gun blast detonated, towing Gabrielle's attention back to the men on the ground.

Both men were strangely still…

No! She threw herself onto her knees next to them. The guy on top—the bad guy—abruptly rolled to the side. Braddock struggled to sit up.

"You scared the hell out of me," Gabrielle snapped.

"But I also saved your life," he reminded, his voice weak but rich with a sense of humor.

Again, she added silently. He'd saved her life again.

But she had saved his, as well.

"I guess we're even," she offered as she helped him to his feet.

"We will be as soon as you get me out of here."

Amy moved into place to help him to his feet. She handed the gun back to Gabrielle without saying anything. Gabrielle understood that she was hinging on the verge of shock. Who wouldn't be after what she'd been through?

When they reached the end of the building, Gabrielle checked the area once more. Clear.

In the distance the wail of sirens had begun.

She wasn't sure how their participation would look to the police or how long it would take to sort through this mess, but she figured it would be best not to get caught anywhere near this chaos.

Braddock stumbled twice before they reached the side gate. Amy rushed ahead and slipped into the guard shack and opened the gate. The three of them made it across the street into the narrow alleyway where Gabrielle had hidden with only seconds to spare before the local authorities descended upon the Fuentes compound.

As badly as she wanted to stop and allow Braddock to rest, she knew they had to put some distance between them and the scene that now looked exactly like a war zone.

The struggle to the far end of the alley was long and arduous. Braddock hadn't spoken since that remark about saving her life and he was leaning more heavily than ever on Gabrielle.

"How you doing, Braddock?" she asked when she could bear the silence no longer.

"Get me to a hospital and I might just live."

As if it had taken his last ounce of strength to answer her question, he fell forward, lugging Amy and Gabrielle down with him.

Gabrielle's heart launched into her throat.

Was he breathing? Had he been shot during that last struggle and she just didn't know it?

Frantic, she surveyed his motionless body. Bruises, scrapes. Dammit. A definite bullet hole.

"I'll stay with him. Go get help," Amy said, her tone flat with exhaustion.

Gabrielle nodded. As she scrambled to her feet, her gaze locked with the other woman's. "Don't let him die."

Amy didn't have to answer, the response was in her eyes. She would try her best.

Traffic moved slowly on the street beyond the end of the alleyway.

Gabrielle burst out of the alley with the intention of stopping a vehicle—any vehicle—at gunpoint.

A Jeep skidded to a stop right in front of her.

Her gaze lit on the driver.

Sloan.

"What took you so long? I've driven around this block twice already."

Chapter Fifteen

Gabrielle sat in the small waiting room without moving or speaking, as she had for the past two hours. Maybe three. She couldn't even guess anymore.

She was too exhausted and too afraid that if she moved or talked or even looked the wrong way that the news would be bad.

Ian Michaels and Ric Martinez had waited in this same room for a while, then when Amy was moved to a room, they apparently both decided to keep her company. They were the people who had arrived at the private airfield and were the reason she'd gotten that ride to where Braddock was being tortured. Thank God they'd come.

That they'd left her here alone was fine with Gabrielle. She had nothing to say to either man. She didn't need Ian to tell her she was fired. She knew she was. Ric had smiled at her, but he was that friendly with everyone. He probably felt sorry for her.

She didn't want anyone feeling sorry for her.

She just wanted Braddock to be okay.

Todd Thompson had called her on the stolen cell phone. She'd almost forgotten she had it. She'd told him she survived and then she'd called numbers in the cell phone's directory until she'd gotten the owner's wife. The phone would be at the hospital's information desk waiting to be picked up. She hadn't wanted to steal it, she'd only needed to borrow it. Kind of like in the movies when a cop or FBI agent confiscated a car for official use.

She doubted the owners of the cell phone would have believed that story, so she hadn't given her name, just the location of the phone.

She hadn't seen Sloan since he'd helped drag Braddock through the ER doors.

Gabrielle was glad Amy was okay. She was banged and bruised, dehydrated and physically exhausted, but otherwise she was holding up. Gabrielle imagined John Calhoun was here by now. From what she'd heard about him, he'd probably started a search party the moment he couldn't get his wife on her cell phone.

If Braddock would just pull through, Gabrielle might have to admit that there was something to this prayer business after all. She'd sure done enough of it in the past two hours. Funny thing, she'd prayed more in the past two or three days than she had in her whole life.

Her whole life.

She was twenty-two, what constituted her entire existence thus far wasn't a hell of a lot.

Most of that time had been less than memorable. She tried to remember back to that time when her mother didn't drink, but she'd been a really little kid and she couldn't recall it that well.

School hadn't been all bad for a girl who was never a cheerleader or team sports participant. She'd never been voted best or favorite anything and she sure hadn't been Miss Popular, but she'd loved learning. Might even have made something of herself if college had worked out.

Sloan was the major reason her adult life had derailed.

That old anger started to churn in her belly. No matter that he'd saved her life, as well as Braddock's and Amy's. The idea that she'd worked with him in any way was just too bizarre.

She closed her eyes and cleared her mind. She was too tired to worry about any of that. Right now her only concern was Braddock.

If he didn't make it…

"Señora."

Gabrielle's eyes flew open. A nurse hovered over her.

"Yes?" Gabrielle was on her feet, her heart pounding, before the woman could blink. "Is he okay?"

The nurse nodded then said in stiff English, "The doctor will explain."

Gabrielle stopped her when she would have gone on her way. "Can I see him?"

"After the doctor explains."

A new wave of worry flooded her. Why would the nurse tell her he was okay and then not allow her to see him until after the doctor explained? Explained what?

The nurse left, probably recognized the signs of the coming meltdown and didn't want to hang around and risk getting caught up in it.

Gabrielle paced. She wore the same clothes she'd had on when she arrived in this country. They were seriously dirty, bloody, as well. She was exhausted and hungry, too, but she didn't care about any of that.

Her weapon had been taken away from her in the ER, as well as her shoulder bag. She was surprised the police hadn't come looking for her considering there had been a small portion of C-4 left in there. Maybe the hospital staff hadn't recognized what it was. The gun they knew.

The door opened again and Gabrielle's heart started racing once more as the doctor appeared.

"Mr. Braddock is doing quite well," he said in perfect English.

Gabrielle glanced at his badge. Dr. Cortez. Maybe he'd gone to school in the States.

"Can I see him?" She needed to see with her own eyes that Braddock was doing well. There were things she wanted to say to him.

"You may see him, but he will be unconscious for some time still."

That was all she needed to hear. "Thanks."

"One moment, Miss Jordan."

She stalled before reaching the door, turned back to the doctor. She hadn't noticed until then just how weary he looked. There was more. She could see it in his eyes.

"Mr. Braddock has four fractured ribs, many, many lacerations and bruises. But the injury that concerned us most was the damaged spleen. We removed the spleen and his condition is finally stable now."

All that she understood. The damaged spleen was serious business but he was okay now. She got it. Her patience was at an end.

"However, his preexisting condition may hinder his recovery somewhat. It is far too early to be certain."

She frowned. Now she was really confused. "I don't understand."

"A copy of Mr. Braddock's medical history was faxed to the hospital by his employer. I'm afraid you will need to ask Mr. Braddock for the details, Miss Jordan."

"I just want to see him." Nothing else mattered right now.

The doctor nodded. "But only briefly. He must rest."

He said nothing more as he escorted her to Braddock's room. A nurse was in the process of checking the barrage of equipment attached to him.

"Five minutes," the doctor said before leaving the room.

The nurse left within seconds of the doctor, leaving Gabrielle alone with Braddock.

She clasped her hands together and approached his bed. He looked even worse now. His face was still swollen and discoloration had set in. But the part that bothered her most was the utter stillness about him.

Her hand trembling, she lay it against his left arm. His skin felt cool. She wondered if she should request a blanket since nothing but a thin sheet covered him from the waist down. An IV was hooked to his right arm while an intimidating-looking monitor tracked his vitals, including his heartbeat, which looked strong and steady.

Tears welled in her throat and it was all Gabrielle could do to hold them back.

This man had reached her on a level she'd thought no one could penetrate. Damn him. He'd touched that place and now she was at a loss as to what to do.

"Idiot," she muttered. One kiss and she was a goner.

What had happened to that tough girl who didn't let anything get to her? How had she lost so much of herself in the past three days without realizing it?

It was all because of him. Her heart squeezed painfully as she stared down at him. Why hadn't he told her about this preexisting health thing? He'd sure as hell known everything about her.

She glanced around the tiny room. White walls and tiled floor. No window. Just a wall of equipment and this bed.

Braddock was one of the good guys. She'd known

that all along. He would, without thought or hesitation, sacrifice himself for others. He'd done that on that mountain and in the compound, even with fractured ribs and a damaged spleen.

Guys like him didn't come along every day.

He was a rare breed. A true hero.

He deserved a hell of a lot better than her.

Her life was way too screwed up for him to salvage.

She imagined going back to jail was on the agenda for her immediate future.

Victoria Colby-Camp would press charges and that would be that.

Not that Gabrielle was feeling sorry for herself or anything. No way. She just understood where her place was in the grand scheme of things, and falling for a man like A.J. Braddock didn't fit.

He deserved better.

"Look, Braddock, I have to go. It's nothing personal," she said, her voice cracking slightly. "But just because you saved my butt a couple of times doesn't mean we have a future. You'll get better." She had to squeeze her eyes shut a moment to hold back the flood of tears brimming behind her lashes.

"You'll go back to the Colby Agency and you won't even miss me."

But I'll sure as hell miss you, she didn't say.

She leaned down and kissed his forehead. It was all she could do to back away.

"So long, Braddock."

She left the room without looking back. She wanted all of this over. Today.

Starting with her business with Sloan.

Gabrielle needn't have worried. The Colby Agency had no intention of letting her forget why she'd come to Mexico in the first place.

Ian Michaels waited outside Braddock's room.

"Martinez will stay here just in case there is any change in his condition," he said. "I'll take you to Victoria."

"Victoria?" She was here? In Mexico?

"She's waiting to talk to you."

As usual, Ian didn't allow his expression or his tone to give away whatever he was thinking. He said what he had to say then turned to lead the way to whatever means of transportation they would be utilizing.

Gabrielle saw no point in asking questions.

He'd already told her what he wanted her to know. And that was that.

IAN DROVE THE SUV and it wasn't until they'd started down that long stretch of desert road that Gabrielle recognized their destination.

Sloan's place.

She noticed the time on the dash and recognized they'd been on the road far longer than she'd realized. She should have anticipated that this was the plan, but she'd been too caught up in worrying about Braddock. Had she done the right thing leaving him that way? Would he really be okay?

Ian didn't speak as he entered a security code at the main gate to Sloan's property and then, using his thumbprint, completed the requirements for entrance.

Gabrielle's emotions whipped into a frenzy as images and sounds of her first visit here tumbled one after the other through her mind.

She got out of the SUV and followed Ian to the door. When it opened, a woman—very attractive, dark hair and eyes—greeted them.

Ian called her Rachel, gave her one of those cheeky hugs, before turning to Gabrielle.

"This is Gabrielle Jordan," he said.

Rachel gifted her with a smile though Gabrielle couldn't tell if it was sincere or not. "Come in, Gabrielle. We've been waiting for you."

As they moved into the house Ian and Rachel discussed how happy they were that A.J. and Amy were both doing well. Rachel assured him that she had gotten an excellent report from her visit to the hospital in the States. On some level Gabrielle followed the conversation, remembering what Mark and Josh had said about Rachel being pregnant, yet she felt oddly detached from the moment. For the first time Gabrielle really looked at the home that belonged to Sloan.

Large but comfortable.

Not cold as she'd expected.

"Gabrielle."

She turned to Rachel. Shook herself back to the present. "Yes?"

"We know you're exhausted and hungry. Come this way and you can relax a bit before meeting with my husband."

Meeting with her husband? Gabrielle thought she was here to see Victoria. She glanced around the entry hall. Ian was already gone. Her gaze landed back on Rachel. Now she was really confused. And why was she being so nice? Didn't she know who Gabrielle was?

"Come."

Rachel ushered her down a long hallway and into a bedroom. "I think you'll find everything you need here. Have a long soak in the tub or take a shower." She gestured to the bed. "I hope these fit." She looked Gabrielle up and down then. "I think you're about the same size as me."

A pair of black slacks and a gray blouse lay on the bed, along with undergarments and even a pair of shoes.

"Seven and a half?" she asked when she noticed Gabrielle's attention on the shoes.

"Seven," Gabrielle allowed, her head spinning with confusion.

"Perhaps they'll do." Rachel smiled again.

Gabrielle hadn't noticed until then that she didn't actually look pregnant. Too early, she supposed.

"I'll check on you again in a bit."

Gabrielle watched her go, still stunned at this turn of events. She looked down at herself and admitted that a shower would definitely be a vast improvement. Fresh clothes would be nice, as well.

For the next half hour she stood under the spray of the hot water. She'd had no idea how badly she needed this until then. When the water started to cool, she reluctantly shut it off and climbed out.

She took her time drying her skin and then her hair. It felt good to be clean. As if she'd washed away a lifetime of dust. And yet some part of her still felt trapped in that past.

The clothes fit a little loosely, but not enough to matter. She'd just closed the last button of the cool silk blouse when a knock on the door interrupted her respite.

Gabrielle opened the door expecting to see Sloan or Victoria and was startled to find Mark, the older of the two boys, standing there holding a tray laden with something that smelled wonderful. Her stomach rumbled.

"May I come in?"

She'd been so taken with the delicious scent she'd forgotten to step back and allow him in. "Sure."

Mark entered, kicked the door closed behind him and walked over to the bed. He set the tray there then perched beside it on the edge of the mattress.

"Do you mind if we talk while you eat?"

Gabrielle shrugged. "It's your house." What could she say? No, you have to go? Besides, she kind of liked the kid. And she could use some company, otherwise she'd start thinking about Braddock again and get all teary-eyed.

Mark let her eat for a while before he said anything, and she deeply appreciated it. The food was amazing. Mixed fruit, spiced rice and something cheesy wrapped in tortillas. And water. Cool, refreshing water.

"I know why you came here."

Her eyes met Mark's. That extraordinary blue color startled her all over again.

"Is that a fact?" she said offhandedly. If Sloan had sent his son in here in an attempt to change her mind about him, he'd wasted his time.

"He wasn't who you think," Mark said without using *his* name.

He didn't have to. Gabrielle understood who he meant.

"I suppose you speak from personal experience," she countered. In spite of her best intentions, her pulse rate had accelerated.

"Yes." He dropped his head, stared at his hands. "The woman who raised me—his sister—wouldn't allow him to see me. She was afraid of what he might do after I got older.

"He hated my father," Mark went on. "Wanted to make him suffer. She worried that he might change his mind about letting her keep me."

Gabrielle's mouth went dry and what was left of her appetite vanished. "She was good to you? This sister." She didn't know why she asked the question. It just felt like the right thing to do.

He nodded. "Yeah. She treated me real good. My father let me stay with her until she died."

"She died?" Gabrielle didn't know that part.

Mark nodded again. "She was really sick when he found out I was still alive, but he didn't want to hurt her since she'd been so good to me. So he let me stay with her until the end."

Gabrielle looked away. Refused to feel any new admiration for the man who'd likely saved her life while helping to rescue Braddock and Amy.

The boy stood. "I should go. Rachel wouldn't want me bothering you." He hesitated at the door. "My brother and I appreciate what you did for us."

She shrugged, too overwhelmed to say much of anything. "No problem."

After he left, Gabrielle stood and restlessly roamed the room. She tried to block Mark's words from her head but they just kept echoing there. She was too tired to think rationally and she knew it.

She needed time and distance to regain some sort of perspective.

Another knock at the door had her pivoting in that direction. She figured this time it would be Victoria to tell her she was fired and going back to prison. Hell, just being across the border was a violation of her parole.

She walked over to the door, braced herself, then opened it.

Sloan.

Her heart rate bumped up a couple beats per second even though she'd known he was going to meet with her.

"I guess it's time we finished our business."

She told herself to speak, to say yes, but a nod was the best she could do.

That intense gaze studied hers a moment. "We'll need some privacy."

With that, he turned and walked away. She followed. He led the way through the house and, oddly, they didn't encounter anyone. Not Ian Michaels or Victoria, Rachel or the boys. All of whom Gabrielle knew were around somewhere.

She imagined they wanted no part of this.

Her gaze settled on the broad shoulders of the man guiding her to what could very well be certain death. Why was he doing this? He'd rescued her...welcomed her into his home and now he was prepared to face off with her?

Outside, the sun was settling behind those rugged mountains she would never forget. Night would come soon and this day would be over.

Where would that leave her?

Sloan stopped at the large structure near the rear

gate she'd decided might be a garage. But she'd been wrong. Inside was a huge workout gym.

But he led her past the mats and equipment to a door that opened into a small break room or something along those lines.

"Sit." He gestured to the table and chairs.

She wondered if that was a good idea. As if she had a choice. She was unarmed. This was his territory. She pulled out a chair and dropped into it.

Sloan opened a cabinet on the other side of the room and took out a bottle of tequila and two glasses. She looked at the label as he sat the bottle on the table and noted that it was the best. She could definitely use a drink.

He filled each glass to the halfway point, slid one toward her and took a long sip from the other.

Just as she started to lift her own glass he reached behind him and withdrew a weapon. Her heart jolted. But instead of aiming at her, he laid the 40-caliber automatic on the table between them. Then he sat down and poured himself more tequila.

Gabrielle downed hers in one long gulp. She placed the empty glass on the table and shook her head when he offered her a refill.

"You came here," he said, those blue eyes boring straight into hers, "to kill me. Is that right?"

Maybe it was the tequila or plain old stupidity, but she found herself nodding.

"Because I killed your father?" he added for clarification.

The words stung through her. Braddock had told her that Sloan hadn't killed her father...was Sloan admitting he had? She didn't want to believe Braddock would lie to her. She blocked thoughts of him, couldn't go there. It hurt too damned much.

"That's right." Surprisingly her voice sounded reasonably strong and steady.

"I didn't kill him," Sloan said bluntly. "But I would have if his girlfriend hadn't."

A volatile mixture of emotions coiled inside her. "Braddock told me that my father killed your wife," she said, her voice shaking with the combination of hurt and anger. "Why would he do that?"

Sloan pushed an envelope in her direction. She blinked to clear her vision, hadn't noticed it lying on the table.

"This is a highly classified file from Interpol. After you've looked at it, you'll need to burn it."

Interpol? She stared at the envelope and then at him. "How do I know this is for real?"

He let go a heavy breath. "I guess you don't." He pushed the weapon a little closer to her. "I'll let you decide for yourself."

She stared at the gun. Was this guy crazy or what? "You think I won't use it?" she demanded, certain that was the real story here.

Sloan propped his arms on the table and leaned

slightly toward her. She resisted the urge to draw away. Not that there was anything at all repulsive about him…he was just intimidating like that.

"The truth is on my side, Miss Jordan," he said in that gravelly voice that would put the fear of God in any breathing human. "I don't have anything to hide from you and I'm damned sure not afraid of you."

She looked at the gun then at the envelope. The idea that he would go to these lengths to prove his point rattled her. Cast a new light on all she'd ever believed.

The way she saw it, she could go on believing hearsay or she could learn the truth. She picked up the envelope and allowed her gaze to shift back up to Sloan's for just a second. It was time to end this. Braddock had told her to weigh the facts.

She opened the envelope and withdrew the documents. Each page was stamped "classified" and clearly marked as having come from Interpol. Even Gabrielle had to admit that this looked like the real deal.

For the next few minutes she lost herself in the file that spelled out what little was known about Gabriel DiCassi. None of it was good. He was, in fact, known as the Angel of Death. He had killed literally dozens of people, including Sloan's first wife. He'd killed Rachel's father. But the most damning evidence of all, in Gabrielle's opinion, was the report on the murder of a prominent couple in Dallas just over twenty-three years ago. A young woman, Lisa Jordan—Gabrielle's mother, the personal assistant of the murdered man—was suspected of having passed along information as to the couple's itinerary that day, but no formal charges had ever been filed.

Gabriel DiCassi had used Lisa to get to his targets just as he had used Rachel to get to her father.

How could she have believed her mother's stories? How could she have lied to Gabrielle that way?

"Don't blame your mother."

She looked up at Sloan, who had apparently read her mind. "How can you say that?" Confusion and anger whirled like a hurricane inside her.

"We all want to believe we're doing the right thing," he said. "Your mother didn't realize who she was dealing with. The fantasies she made up afterward were a self-defense mechanism. They weren't meant to hurt you, just to protect herself." He shrugged. "And maybe you."

Gabrielle shook her head. None of this had been about her. "But she kept in contact with him after that…how could she do that when she knew what he had done?"

"It was part of the fantasy. She needed to believe she hadn't done anything wrong."

Gabrielle tossed the papers aside, couldn't read or listen to any more. "I don't want to know this."

"You need to know the truth so you can get on with your life."

She laughed, disgusted with herself for being such a

fool, mad at him for pointing it out. "My life is over, or didn't you know that? I'm probably going back to prison. I screwed up the best chance anyone ever gave me."

Sloan smiled. Gabrielle wondered if maybe the tequila was paying havoc with her ability to properly process what she saw and heard. Why would he smile at her misery?

"If our business is finished," he said, "I think you have some unfinished issues with Victoria, as well."

Gabrielle had almost forgotten that Victoria was here.

Sloan indicated the weapon. "Are you going to need this?"

She looked from the gun to the man. She'd definitely never met anyone like him. "No." It was true. The business between them was finished. She abruptly felt as if a massive weight had been lifted from her shoulders. Years and years of unfounded emotional baggage. All because she'd believed her mother's fantasies. But there was a gaping hole left behind.

"Good." He stood and picked up the weapon. "Victoria would like to speak with you now." He nodded toward the tequila. "Feel free to brace yourself."

Gabrielle swallowed hard and summoned her courage. As tempting as his suggestion was, she needed a clear head.

Gabrielle stood as Sloan left the break room or conference room, whatever it was. Victoria walked through the door next. Gabrielle estimated that if she could face Sloan and survive it, she could face this. Her mind was still reeling with all she'd learned.

Victoria gestured to Gabrielle's chair before settling into the one Sloan had vacated. "I won't waste your time, Gabrielle."

She tensed, hadn't really expected idle chitchat, but it might have been nice. Gabrielle sat again.

"What you did was wrong. I gave you the opportunity to join the ranks of the best and you took advantage of the situation."

"Yes," Gabrielle admitted. "I did. And, believe it or not, that's one of the things I'm most sorry for." Just another lesson learned a little too late.

"You're not getting off with a mere apology," Victoria attested, her expression stern.

Gabrielle hadn't expected to. "I understand."

"Of course," Victoria went on, "I will permit you to take a brief break to reevaluate your life before reporting back to work."

Stunned, Gabrielle echoed, "Reporting back to work?"

"I've never been wrong about an investigator, Gabrielle. I'm not about to let you be the first blemish on that record." That stern expression softened into a smile. "You'll make an excellent investigator. Is two weeks sufficient time for you to regroup?"

Gabrielle couldn't answer right away. She was too

shocked, too overcome. She'd expected a one-way ticket back to prison. She gave herself a mental shake. Victoria was waiting for a response. "I appreciate your confidence in me," she responded, finally managing to string the words together.

Victoria stood. "I'll take that as a ycs. I'll see you in two weeks."

With that, she left. Gabrielle was too stunned to do anything but watch her go.

Well, at least now she knew...there really was something to that whole prayer thing.

She had herself a second chance for a real future.

Chapter Sixteen

Two weeks later

It felt strange to be back in her Chicago apartment. When Gabrielle had left she'd assumed she would never see the place again.

But that had been before.

Everything had changed now.

As Victoria suggested, she had spent the past two weeks regrouping. She'd gone back to her hometown in Texas and visited her mother's grave. She'd dropped by her old high school and even the house where she'd grown up.

All of it felt like another life now.

She'd contacted the Interpol agent listed in the documents Sloan had given her and learned even more about the man her father had been.

Just how wrong she had been still startled her. Her

mother's stories were just what Sloan said, self-preservation fantasies.

But Gabrielle had worked past that. She'd forgiven her mother and herself for being fools. Life was too short to waste any more of it.

She'd contacted Amy a week ago to check on her. She was doing fine, resting at home and letting her husband take care of her. Amy had told her that Braddock was home and doing well, also. He was going back to work soon.

Tomorrow, when Gabrielle returned to the Colby Agency, she would have to face Braddock…as well as the others. It would take a long time for her to regain trust. Despite Victoria having given her this second chance, she understood that the others might not be so quickly forgiving. She'd lied to them, had threatened one of their own.

She drew in a deep breath. But she could do this. She was strong. She wasn't afraid to answer for her mistakes.

The only part that worried her just a little was running into Braddock. She wasn't sure she could pretend that how he felt didn't affect her.

She'd pretty much fallen in love with the guy. It was dumb, she knew. He was older, smarter and far too good for her. At any rate, she couldn't help how she felt. The question was, could she keep her cool and not do anything embarrassing or stupid?

Gabrielle pushed away the troubling thoughts and considered her apartment. When she'd leased the place she'd intended it to be temporary. Now that she was back, she'd have to consider redecorating. A little paint, if the landlord would permit it. Some artwork and definitely some new furniture.

A smile tilted her lips. She could afford it. Being a Colby Agency investigator paid well. Better than she'd ever dreamed of making.

A new car might be in order, as well. Why not go all out, right?

Her doorbell rang and she almost jumped out of her skin. Who in the world? Amy, maybe? No, Thompson. He'd said he might stop by. He was glad to hear that she was coming back. The other new recruit that had been hired with them had resigned, unable to handle the rigors of the job. That left just the two of them to pave the way for new blood, Thompson insisted.

Gabrielle opened the door, hoping he'd picked up pizza before stopping by.

Not Thompson. Her brain registered what her eyes saw and left her speechless.

Braddock.

The swelling was gone from his face as was most of the discoloration. But there was a definite new, ever so slight angle to his nose that hadn't been there before.

Man, did he look good.

"Hello."

She realized then that she'd been staring and hadn't even said hello. "Hey."

"You mind if I come in?"

Where was her brain? "No. Sure. Come in." She backed up and opened the door wider.

He walked with a bit of a limp and her heart squeezed painfully.

She closed the door and struggled to restrain the damned tears that instantly brimmed on her lashes. She had to keep her cool here. Whatever his reason for stopping by, she couldn't let him see how pathetic she was.

She faced him, pushed a smile into place. "You look great." Her gaze swept the length of him. Crisp button-down shirt, well-worn jeans. All fit him as if they'd been designed especially for his great body.

"I'm better."

She reminded herself to breathe. "So what brings you by?" She winced. She hadn't meant for it to sound as if she didn't appreciate his stopping by, she was just a little confused and a whole lot nervous.

His gaze settled on hers and the breath she'd struggled to take in left her in a rush. "I wanted to apologize," he said quietly, that deep voice making her shiver. God she did love to listen to him talk.

Apologize? "You don't owe me any apology." How could he think he had anything to apologize for? That was ridiculous. She dared to move away from the door just a little, putting her closer to him.

"I rationalized my actions by telling myself that if I got sick it would ruin both our lives. So I ignored my feelings, pretended I wasn't interested in a romantic relationship. I stayed away from intimate entanglements period. I let you get away when maybe, if I'd done the right thing, maybe I could have helped you through this instead of just standing back and doing nothing."

He blamed himself for her stupidity? "This wasn't your fault, Braddock," she argued. "You couldn't have known what I had in mind. This was my quest, my mistake." She wanted to know more about his health, but let him get to it in his own time.

He took a step closer…wrapped the long, gentle fingers of his hands around her arms. It was all she could do not to throw herself into his strong arms. She'd dreamed of him holding her again…of that kiss.

"If I'd followed my instincts and let myself get close to you, maybe I could have made you feel something besides the need for revenge."

Did this mean he'd felt something for her before? "You had feelings for me before that trek in the mountains?" She'd known she was attracted to him…who was she kidding? She'd been infatuated with him.

"Definitely." He smiled and her heart lurched. "I know we both have to go back to work tomorrow, but I'm hoping we can, taking our time, of course, see where this leads us. If you can deal with the reality that my future is a little less than certain." He explained about the immune disorder caused by the virus.

She couldn't take any more. She threw her arms around his neck and went on tiptoe to brush a kiss across his lips. "Don't sweat the future, Braddock. None of us is guaranteed tomorrow. Nothing is certain. I just learned that the hard way." She nipped his lower lip with her teeth. He shuddered. "And, maybe you older guys like to take things slow, but girls my age, we don't like to waste time."

"I think I can handle that," he murmured.

And then he kissed her...long and deep. With her entire being she knew that this kiss would never, ever be enough.

She drew back, slid her hands down to his and entwined her fingers there. "We need to take up where we left off."

He looked confused for a moment. Gorgeous and utterly confused.

"You know," she prompted, "with you on top."

A grin spread across his face. "I hope you have something other than a rocky hole in the ground in mind."

She walked backward, tugging him toward her bedroom. "I have this amazing bed with pink silk sheets."

"Pink?" he teased.

She nodded. "It's my one girlie fetish. I love sleek, pink sheets."

By the time they reached her bed they'd stripped off one another's clothes. And seconds after that he was on top, right where she wanted him. She moaned with satisfaction. Loved the feel of his skin against hers. Adored the taste of his lips. But most of all she loved him.

He pushed inside her, bonding them heart and soul, taking them both to a place that would forever be theirs.

Complete happiness.

**Hidden in the secrets of antiquity,
lies the unimagined truth...**

Introducing

a brand-new line filled with mystery
and suspense, action and adventure,
and a fascinating look into history.

And it all begins with DESTINY.

In a sealed crypt in
France, where the
terrifying legend of
the beast of Gevaudan
begins to unravel,
Annja Creed discovers
a stunning artifact
that will seal her destiny.

*Available every other
month starting
July 2006, wherever
you buy books.*

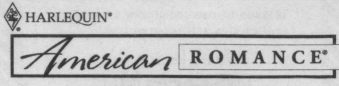

HARLEQUIN®

American **ROMANCE®**

IS THRILLED TO BRING YOU A
HEARTWARMING MINISERIES BY
BESTSELLING AUTHOR

Judy Christenberry

Children of TEXAS

Separated during childhood, five siblings from the
Lone Star state are destined to rediscover one another,
find true love and a build a Texas-sized family legacy
they can call their own....

You won't want to miss the fifth and
final installment of this beloved family saga!

VANESSA'S MATCH
On sale June 2006 (HAR#1117)

Also look for:

REBECCA'S LITTLE SECRET
On sale September 2004 (HAR#1033)

RACHEL'S COWBOY
On sale March 2005 (HAR#1058)

A SOLDIER'S RETURN
On sale July 2005 (HAR#1073)

A TEXAS FAMILY REUNION
On sale January 2006 (HAR #1097)

This riveting new saga begins with

In the Dark

by national bestselling author

JUDITH ARNOLD

The party at Hotel Marchand is in full swing when the lights suddenly go out. What does head of security Mac Jensen do first? He's torn between two jobs—protecting the guests at the hotel and keeping the woman he loves safe.

A woman to protect. A hotel to secure. And no idea who's determined to harm them.

On Sale June 2006

HARLEQUIN®

INTRIGUE®

COMING NEXT MONTH

#921 AUTOMATIC PROPOSAL by Kelsey Roberts
Miami Confidential

Three years ago, Luke Young was left at the altar when DEA agent Julia Garcia broke cover to take down a drug trafficker. But when she reenters his life, there's no way things can ever go back to the way they were. Except for the stray bullets, explosions and renewed attempts on both their lives.

#922 DREAM WEAVER by Jenna Ryan

Someone, somewhere, keeps giving Meliana Maynard white roses. Will FBI agent Johnny Grand be able to uncover her admirer before this affection blossoms into something less innocent?

#923 MY SISTER, MYSELF by Alice Sharpe
Dead Ringer

When Tess Mays discovers she has an identical twin, she thinks her life is finally coming together. But with her sister in a coma, Tess stumbles knee-deep into an arson investigation, assuming her sister's identity to clear the name of a father she never knew.

#924 SLATER HOUSE by Patricia Rosemoor

When Melanie Pierce travels to her family's ancestral home against her mother's wishes, she stands to inherit a fortune. But she soon discovers the estate hides secrets—and bodies—in every room. Architect Ross Bennet seems to know a great deal about the Slater family's tragic past, but will Mel soon become part of it?

#925 SERIAL BRIDE by Ann Voss Peterson
Wedding Mission

Sylvie Hayes went looking for her sister, thinking she only had cold feet, but instead found a torn wedding veil stained with blood. Attorney Bryce Walker's skyrocketing career was halted by one brash mistake. Each believed the same man was responsible for these terrible events in their lives. But if serial killer Dryden Kane was in prison, who was doing all the killing?

#926 FORBIDDEN TERRITORY by Paula Graves

Lily Browning has a gift that allows her to see the terrible things no one else does. But when Lily runs from her visions in pursuit of a normal life, she runs right into police detective J. McBride. But in his eyes, all Lily sees is a lost, lonely little girl. Will she be able to help him reclaim the part of himself that vanished so long ago?